THE LONG BALL

ARIA COLE

Mich enjoy the long ball!

xo Aria

The star player with a troubled past…
Cash Greenwood escaped a difficult past by becoming a star baseball player. Now, one of the major league's rare double threats, all his effort is thrown into the sport. He's never had any interest in women, until he meets the one woman who wants nothing to do with him.

The daughter of baseball royalty…
Delilah Gray's life revolves around numbers, research, and data. She has no time for anything messy like emotions or relationships. Especially not when they come in the sexy guise of a baseball player. She's seen first-hand the devastation caused by dating a man obsessed with the sport, and that's one risk she's not willing to take.

She is one curveball he never saw coming…
But this is one pitch Cash is determined to hit out of the park. Sexual tensions run high and feelings start to develop, but will Delilah ever see that they could have a solid future together? Determined to make her his, she may just prove to be the hardest game of Cash's life.

WARNING: The Long Ball features an obsessed jock with six-pack abs in tight pants determined to get his girl. If syrupy sweet romance and fiery passions appeal to you, then hold onto your panties because this one may just hit them out of the park.

To Sybil,

Thank you for always helping me nail it. I would be naked without you.

All my love,

Aria

Introduction

The star player with a troubled past...
Cash Greenwood escaped a difficult past by becoming a star baseball player. Now, one of the major league's rare double threats, all his effort is thrown into the sport. He's never had any interest in women, until he meets the one woman who wants nothing to do with him.

The daughter of baseball royalty...
Delilah Gray's life revolves around numbers, research,

and data. She has no time for anything messy like emotions or relationships. Especially not when they come in the sexy guise of a baseball player. She's seen first-hand the devastation caused by dating a man obsessed with the sport, and that's one risk she's not willing to take.

She is one curveball he never saw coming...
But this is one pitch Cash is determined to hit out of the park. Sexual tensions run high and feelings start to develop, but will Delilah ever see that they could have a solid future together? Determined to make her his, she may just prove to be the hardest game of Cash's life.

WARNING:
The Long Ball features an obsessed jock with six-pack abs in tight pants determined to get his girl. If syrupy sweet romance and fiery passions appeal to you, then hold onto your panties because this one may just hit them out of the park.

Prologue

Cash

I always get asked the question, *what's the best part about playing baseball?* How do you explain the feeling of flying? People associate flying with freedom, so that's an easy answer, but it's so much more than that. Flying makes it seem like nothing matters; the world just slips away and the only feeling that remains is the euphoria from spreading your wings.

When I'm on the plate and waiting for that ball to whip by and connect with my bat, I'm the ruler of my universe. I'm in control. I'm in the driver's seat. A stadium packed with sixty-thousand fans, watching, waiting. Normally loud, boisterous, full of gumption and occasionally way too much testosterone, but suddenly they are all silent, waiting with bated breath—waiting on me. And that anticipation…oh, that anticipation is sweeter than anything else.

My heart races, exhilarates, then explodes. I feel my body both bunch with nerves and stand tall in pride as that ball comes and connects with the bat, now an extension of myself.

The fans yell in abandon.

They see it, the long ball…

1

Cash

"Stop being a whiny bitch, Greenwood! Bottoms up!"

My best friend and resident troublemaker of the team smacked me on the back. His boisterous laugh and booming voice took up all the space around him. I loved many things about the man, but the thing I loved the most was that in his presence, I became invisible. Since the age of 16 I've been recognizable. Once you were a star athlete with a future and the hope of winning a championship, you became a commodity, something shiny. And being simultaneously a slugger and a pitcher was a combination so rare that those with it, like myself, were priceless.

It hadn't taken me long to learn that being invisible keeps you safe.

"We have to meet that analytics chick in an hour. I don't want to reek of alcohol. Coach will kick our asses." I didn't like to drink. Most days I couldn't even stomach the smell of it, but for the sake of keeping up appearances I usually nursed a glass in my hand and always offered to be the designated driver so no one suspected anything. Rod was really good about covering for me when needed, chugging back the drinks people often bought for me, acting like the cocky best friend he was.

"It's still technically the off-season. Another one won't hurt."

"Another always hurts, particularly in the form of a hangover the next morning," I replied.

"You sound like a dodgy old fuck. Where's the guy who used to party with me all night long? I want him back."

I chuckled, thinking about all the times we'd been in trouble. I prided myself on how well I blended into the crowd and let him take the attention. Rodriguez and I had been buddies since our rookie year. We'd grown up together on this team, cut our teeth on the ins and outs of playing professional ball, but as time passed I found that faking it seemed to exhaust me more and more each day. I was tired of it all, and the only thing that still made me feel something was the game. Everything else was endless noise that passed by with no true meaning or intention. I felt like I was walking in a blur, just waiting for time to pass.

"I'm not twenty-one anymore. Coach said any more stunts like that one you pulled at warm-ups and we're both benched. And you, motherfucker, are not getting me benched." The idea of sitting out a game was unbearable. Rod and I were thick as thieves, and Coach knew that if anyone could reel him in, it would be me. But what the coach didn't know was that the idea of losing baseball in any way was like a noose around my neck, tightening until all the oxygen was ripped from me.

"You're my wingman, buddy, and ya gotta admit, spiking the water cooler was pretty genius."

"And landed us in a shit load of trouble. Frankly, I'm just too old for this shit anymore. Let the rookies have at it. We had our fun."

"You make thirty sound like a death sentence. Not for me. When I turn the big 3-0 next year I'm going big. I want my feet in the sand with a drink in my hand and a pussy on each arm. Fuck it, a limo full of pussy. I am gonna get more ass that night than a toilet seat."

"Yeah, I bet you do." I'd never liked how Rodriguez embraced the cliché ball player persona. He played ball hard—out on the field he was a beast. But he partied even harder, a revolving door of girls after every game. I was always up for a few drinks, but the groupies that surrounded Rodriguez always made my stomach turn. It was so obvious they wanted him for his status and money —his staggering salary was very appealing to bunt bunnies. I had absolutely zero interest in them.

All the women around ball players didn't have much to offer, and my life was so messed up that I doubt any woman wanted anything to do with it when she found out. The only kind that would stay would be one that would hope for a staggering payday at the end. I had enough people standing by with their hand out, so I wasn't interested in a woman who wanted that, too.

11

Besides, I only had a few more years to play this game, and I wasn't going to squander them for some chick. These women didn't care about the men. They cared about the limos, the big ticket items the ball players paid for, and the thousand-dollar dinners. Rodriguez made hundreds of millions, just like so many of my buddies, and just like the other ball players, he had no issue living like a king. But that lifestyle didn't interest me in the least.

This life wasn't for everyone, I wasn't even sure it was for me sometimes. I rarely liked to go out, and the women did nothing for me. I lived and breathed the game, so much so that I couldn't imagine what else I would be doing if it wasn't this. I had one single focus and that was to win the World Series. I had been playing ball for eleven years with the MLB, and that was the only thing that eluded me. I was known as the best player in the entire league and yet I didn't have that World Series title under my belt. My years left playing ball were dwindling—a ball player was gettin' some age by thirty —but it was the one dream I hadn't yet attained.

"Let's head over, man. Don't want to piss off Coach."

Rod slammed his shot glass down on the counter, his eyes shining with excitement. "Wanna place bets on how fast I can get up the analytic girl's skirt?"

"You haven't even seen her yet." We walked out the doors of the corner bar, afternoon light heating my skin as we walked the short block to the stadium. Today we had a meeting with what would be the new official star analytics firm for the club, before opening day tomorrow. I'd been waiting months for this day, the time between playoffs and opening season always left a pit of dread in my stomach. If I could play twelve months of the year I would.

We pushed through the stadium doors and made our way down the dim hallway, headed for the conference room next to the locker room. I nodded at Coach when we walked in and greeted a few of the other guys as the entire team settled on benches around the center of the room.

"I don't want to take up much of your time, so I'll cut right to the chase." Coach looked around the room. "A few of you have been fucking off, so we need focus if we're going to have a good season. I don't expect miracles, but I do expect you to listen. No more antics. Stay focused. I expect each of you to improve your averages by the end of the season. "

"Like it or not, stats are down, guys. We need all heads in the game if we're gonna improve and have a shot at going all the way this year. Delilah Grey from Lionsgate Analytics is here to help us do that. She'll be with us—every game, every day—all season. She'll be sending me the stats throughout the game, and I want you guys tuned in to your averages. Push yourselves every night." He glanced around the room, pausing for a moment on Rod. "And please treat Delilah with respect. She knows we need some help, but she doesn't need to know you're all a bunch of animals." God, I loved Coach. So steady and calm. He was the reason this team was great. Without him we'd all be a bunch of animals on the field.

Coach swung open the locker room door and in walked a fucking vision.

I noticed the heels first. Sexy stilettos with leather cutouts that made me want to get down on my knees and slip them off her feet one at a time. My eyes devoured her creamy, toned calves, and not even the conservative pencil skirt could hide the full curves of her hips.

"Jesus," Rod said under his breath.

I nudged him, for the first time in my life irritated by his overt appreciation of a woman. Looking at Delilah, the hairs on my arms stood to attention. As did something else. Damn, she was stunning, I'd never seen a woman so radiant in my entire life. She had dark silky hair cascading down her back in loose curls, so damn soft-looking that my hand itched to brush up against them. I, Cash Greenwood, for the first time in my life, had a desire to brush up against a woman's hair.

"Hey guys, I'm Delilah Grey." She nodded, her spine rigid as she leafed through a handful of papers in her arms. "If you could pass these around, I'll tell you a little about me, then we can chat individually."

"Individually?" Rod chimed, his horny grin sending anger racing through my stomach.

"Yes, that's how I prefer to work. Deal with each player's specific issues before we bring the whole team together."

"I've only got one issue." Rod shifted in his seat, his hand brushing over his crotch. My nostrils flared. Why was he such a dick? At that moment I hated my best friend so much I wanted to pound his face into the ground. The thought made me feel ashamed and idiotic. I knew Rod, he was a joker, more talk than action on most days, but the fact that he was being crass to this woman upset me beyond all reason. I didn't have an explanation, but I did not enjoy the idea of Rod looking at her like she was a piece of meat. Not one bit.

Delilah's deep chocolate eyes narrowed in a flare of anger for a moment before she turned back to her paperwork. If one paid close attention to her, as I was doing, one could see the patch of red forming on the back of her neck. "I started Lionsgate Analytics nearly three years ago. I want you to be the best players, on and off the field, and excelling in this world isn't just about home runs and fly balls. It's also about measuring, distance, velocity, and spin rates." Her eyes flicked over the team again. "I'll be hanging out at all the games, laptop open and watching just how consistent everyone is, and hopefully it won't take us long to get an average. Anyone have questions for me?"

"Yeah, got plans tonight, sweetheart?" That was Rod, and I nearly shoved my fist in his gut for that one. I watched as Delilah's jaw ticked. She was tough, I could tell. I liked that. I liked that she wouldn't take anything sitting down. I had had enough of women taking things sitting down, so the fighter in me was drawn to the fire in her.

"Let me make one other thing clear: if anyone calls me sweetheart, toots, doll, baby, or any other demeaning term of endearment again, I can't promise you won't feel my high heel in your balls. I don't play well with men who act like animals. We're here for one thing and one thing only—to get this team in shape to win this year. I'd appreciate it if you didn't make an ass out of yourself in the process. Have I made myself clear?"

Fire blazed through my veins when she spun and exited the very door she'd come from. Well damn, after thirty years I finally found a woman who could make me take notice, make me want to chase. And not only chase, but tie her up and hold her against me, bind her to me in every way possible.

"Well, glad that went well." Coach pushed a hand through his graying hair. "Cash, you go first."

I followed her out of the room and into the smaller suite next door. When I entered she was already seated at the small desk, a few papers spread out before her, arms crossed over her chest as she waited. I licked my lips when I saw her. God, she was something else, all hard and edgy but yet so soft and delicate at the same time. She was wearing a crisp, white, button-down shirt under her blazer, and although she wasn't showing any skin, I knew that the pretty packaging was nothing compared to the delectable gift of her flesh. She had her shirt buttoned almost to her chin, but that only made me want to pop those buttons with my teeth and peel the fabric off her body, exploring every inch of her with my tongue as I went.

I shook my head to clear the images of her naked body displayed before me, a wonderland waiting for me to enter, and I sat down, rather uncomfortably, in the seat across from her.

"Cash Greenwood?" She held up a sheet of paper, my black-and-white team photo printed across the top.

"That's me." I crossed my arms, relaxing back into my chair as I watched her with an interested eye.

"Why do you think Coach asked me to sit down with you?"

"Because he asked everyone to?"

Her eyes flickered at my smart reply. She sucked in a quick breath, her chest heaving with the movement and stretching the fabric across her round, sexy tits. I wondered if she was wearing a push-up bra, but then figured there was no way tits that beautiful could be a slight of hand.

"Because you're the pitcher. The pitcher tends to be the natural-born leader, and according to these stats…"

She glanced down at the sheet of paper. "You're the star hitter, too. You have any idea how rare your talent is?" She arched an eyebrow. "So is there anything you want to start with, beyond a smart-ass remark?"

A deep grin pulled at my cheeks as I held her eyes, letting the silence stretch between us until she started squirming in her chair. I made her nervous. I bit down on my bottom lip as my eyes flicked up and down her body before I finally spoke. "Maybe I was hoping you could teach me a thing or two."

Why the fuck did I just do that?

I wanted to kick my own ass. I sounded like a waste-of-space asshole jock, one who thinks he can do whatever and act however just because he plays baseball. Like some instinct kicked in, I'd wanted to protect myself, and acting like a dick meant that no one would try to penetrate the shell I had set into place so very long ago.

Delilah's cheeks flamed, the crimson crawling right up her neck and making me wish I could see what the rest of her looked like when she blushed. I liked the idea of her being flushed red based on something I'd said. I wondered if her nipples were the same shade as her petal-pink lips, and what the weight of her heavy tits in my hands would feel like. Jesus, I sounded like Rod, because this kind of thinking sure as hell wasn't me.

"You may be used to girls fawning all over you, pulling up their skirts with one cocky grin, but save your breath, hot shot. I'm not that girl, and I never will be. Now, if you're done with the eye-fucking, can we get on to business?"

Her reply swept the air from my lungs. She certainly wasn't that girl, and that's exactly why she'd caught my interest. She wasn't impressed by any of the talent on this team, including mine, but I'm a man who likes a challenge. And Delilah Grey was one hell of a challenge.

"To answer your question, no, there isn't anything I want to say to you. I'm not the guy who should be in this seat."

"And who do you think is?"

"Coach called you in after Rodriguez fucked up. Look, he's my best friend, I'm not going to bullshit you. He isn't a bad guy. He means well. He just likes to have fun. Every team needs that guy, and Rod is that guy. He keeps spirits up. I know you're here because Coach thinks the partying has slowed us down, and I think it's a great idea. Get the guys focused on their stats, challenging themselves and bettering their game. I think it's a good plan, but don't be too hard on Rod. His heart's in the game. That's the part that counts." Sometimes he drinks too much, and that affects his game. I didn't want to share that with her, but it was obvious that's what was going on. Rod's drinking was out of hand, but at least he showed up to practice and never lost his temper. He wasn't an angry drunk, and that at least was something in my book.

Delilah leaned back in her chair, eyes burning up the space between us before she swept her long dark hair over one shoulder. It fell down past the full swell of her breast, and the only thing I could think of was getting a look at all those dark tresses against the creamy flesh of her naked body.

"So if you don't think you need me, why are you here then?"

"Because you interest me." I was unable to keep the wide grin from my face.

A wry smile cut across her full lips. Fuck, I wanted to

bite those lips. I wanted to trace her curves under my palms and push my hands in her hair, kiss her so fucking hard that when we'd finish we'd both be gasping for air. "Well, I've got news for you, Cash Greenwood. I hate ball players. You couldn't pay me to date one. You're all the same, and I have no desire to get swept up in your bullshit. I'm here to help the team out, and I guarantee I'll be gone just as soon as my job is done. Just between you and me, I refused this job three times, but your coach begged me, so here I am."

"Christ, you're beautiful when you're angry." I couldn't believe I'd just said that. I'd wanted to say something witty, but all I could think about was how her beauty took my breath away, so I'd said it. I'd called her beautiful.

Her mouth opened and closed, shock lacing the features of her pretty face. "Excuse me?"

"I said you're beautiful when you're angry. I didn't know a person could be, I usually just think of pinched faces and ruddy cheeks, but the way your nose crinkles —"

"Okay, stop." She stood from her chair, sending it sliding on the floor behind her. Her eyes were wild, the fire burning bright behind her irises, her chest heaving with exasperated pants before she put a hand on one hip and pointed to the door with her other hand. "It's been a pleasure, Greenwood. Send the next caveman in, if you could."

"Caveman?" I stood, hands planted on the desk in front of me as I leaned across the table, shortening the distance between us. "I can't speak for the rest of the guys, but I'm definitely not a caveman. Give me a little time and you might even find I surprise you." The fact that she lumped me in with all men bothered me. I didn't want her thinking that I was one of these assholes who used women like they were nothing, then disregarded them.

"Doubt it."

"I don't." I paused, eyes riveted on her pretty deep brown ones. The air hung heavy with a heady mix of arousal and irritation.

"I'll see you tomorrow, Greenwood."

"I'm looking forward to it."

"I'm not."

"Ya know, for a girl who hates baseball players so much, I find it odd you're spending the next few months living and breathing it."

Her jaw worked back and forth at my words, her eyes falling to my cocky grin, then back to my eyes. "Yeah, well, it's complicated."

I waited, hoping she'd elaborate. I was desperate to find out why she had such a chip on her shoulder. Hell, I was desperate to spend more time with her, period.

"Enjoy the rest of your night, Ms. Grey." I winked when I pushed off the table, her frown deepening as her thighs shifted back and forth beneath that sexy power suit. I left the room with two thoughts running through my head: what would it look like if she was wearing nothing but those heels, and how would they feel digging in my back?

"Man, Grey has a stick up her ass," Rod commented as we left the clubhouse nearly three hours later. Apparently Delilah had lain into him, not that he didn't deserve it.

"I think it's hot." And I did. I was used to these

women who would do anything I said whenever I said it. This one, though, was a hard ass. I liked the embers that burned in her, the inferno under the librarian get-up and cold stance. This girl was a fighter.

"What?! Fuck that, I don't like working for my dinner."

I shook my head, shoving my hands in my pockets and fishing out my keys. Rod and I had driven together because we lived in the same high-rise.

"Since when have you ever liked the idea of any woman?" he scoffed as we approached my car.

"Just because I don't eat up the chicks that fall all over you doesn't make me blind. It makes me selective. I don't want a Big Mac when I could have a filet mignon."

"Pussy is pussy. No one is looking at the mantle when they're poking a fire. You're a Timberwolf, man. Enjoy the spoils." Rod humped the air in a juvenile gesture. Some days I'm shocked that he's my best friend.

"Delilah wasn't wrong when she called you a caveman." I shook my head.

"Caveman? Fuck, she's a barracuda. I'm a great guy! Do you know anyone who doesn't think I'm the life of the party?"

"Aside from every woman you've ever met?"

"No, people that really know me."

"People don't really know you, man. You put so much noise out there—"

"Hey, whose side are you on here?" Rod cut me an irritated look.

"I'm not taking sides. Just not feelin' the young, drunk, dumb, and full of cum vibe anymore." That statement wasn't fair. Rod had been there for me whenever I needed him, no questions asked. He had his faults, but the man was loyal, and I knew that if I needed him for anything he would be there. But just like everyone else, he had his own demons.

"Oh, look at your holier-than-thou ass. Spare me, Cash. Spare me."

I shook my head as we pulled out of the parking garage, heading for our building, where I could thankfully drop his ass off and enjoy my last night alone for a long time. After this it was all double headers and late nights for me.

"Wanna order pizza tonight?"

"Nah, I'm gonna get some rest." I pushed a hand through my hair, my thoughts still on Delilah Grey and her long dark hair. Would it be inappropriate to invite her to my place for a one-on-one session? Because I really fucking wanted to. I didn't know what had gotten into me, but as soon as I saw her, I'd tucked my balls right into her purse. Now I just had to figure out how to get her to give me the time of day.

No one had ever made me feel the things she'd made me feel down deep in my gut when she'd walked into the room. I'd wanted to haul her off over my shoulder and steal her back to my place. Sure, I had caveman tendencies, but I did a pretty good job at keeping them to myself. Until now. Until her.

"Maybe Gina is around tonight." Rod pulled out his phone and tapped out a text to his long-standing on-again-off-again fuck-buddy. Gina was a good girl. She really liked him, I could tell, and Rod liked her, too. He may want to deny it, but Rod had found the one. I just hoped he could get his shit together before she walked away.

"You should be good to her, man. Take her out or

something."

"Nah." He shook his head adamantly. "Gina's too good for me. I'd never tie her down with my bullshit." Rod's demons held him in place. He was so scared to let a woman in that he just pushed away every girl he could possibly care for. He didn't think he deserved someone kind or decent. If he didn't stop, he was going to push the only girl that he cared about right out the door.

"Maybe cut the bullshit. She likes you. I don't know why she likes you, but she does."

"I'm too busy to be tied down." He was typing again. The dumb fool wanted to be tied down, but his past just kept him running away instead of toward something. We had a similar past, except mine kept me closed off, and his kept him too open but never invested. "Sweet, Gina's coming over in an hour. If you hear screams, don't be alarmed."

I shook my head, finding my best friend completely fucking hopeless, and yet still he managed to make me smile.

"And that's why you're a caveman."

Rod rolled his eyes as I pulled the car into my reserved parking space.

"At least this caveman gets laid once in awhile."

"Once in awhile? I'm surprised your dick hasn't fallen off from overuse. How you don't have a fucking STD is beyond me. I hope you wrap that dick up before you use it."

"Not this dick, man. I've got some serious endurance. And yes, *asshole*, I always wrap up little Rod. Big Daddy takes care of his little man." Rod grabbed his cock, grinning like a moron as we stepped into the elevator.

"Jesus, what the fuck does Gina see in you? You are a

fucking moron. You are twenty-nine and just gave your junk a nickname. Tell her I say hi and she should dump your ass." I punched the button for the penthouse.

He paused for a minute as the elevator whirred up eighteen floors. "Join us if you get bored. Loads of pizza, and Gina says you're sweet, not like the other buffoons on the team, so you're welcome anytime. Just don't touch her, man. She is off limits."

I laughed at the vehemence in his voice, Rod may have wanted to deny it, but Gina had him by the balls.

"Thanks, man. I think I'm in for the night, though. Leftovers and a baseball game."

"You know, you really should find yourself a girl, Greenwood. Someone to go home to at night instead of spending all that time alone. Or better yet, a hot piece of ass that will come on over and just fuck your brains out."

I nodded, turning his words over in my head. I did want that. I wanted a good woman and kids running around under my feet. But I didn't want what I'd had as a kid. No way did I want that for any kid of mine. "Thanks for the advice, caveman."

He nodded, the doors sliding open once we'd come to a stop. "Later, bro."

"Later," I called as the doors whirred closed. Never had I been so thankful to be alone in my life. I realized, though, that I longed for her company. I'd be more than happy to spend time with Delilah Grey any day of the week.

2

Delilah

"So I fisted her ass in both my hands, slammed her against my front door, and right there in the hallway, man, her hands go for my di—"

"Hey, boys," I chimed in just before one of the players went into a graphic story about his latest sexual conquest.

"Ms. Grey." The players' eyes roamed up and down my body, sending a painful shiver through me. Baseball players are douchebags. I never thought I'd find myself here, behind the scenes and working with these rowdy, testosterone-injected jocks. But the coach was an old family friend and I couldn't exactly say no, and for a former ball player he was a decent guy—married since he was twenty-one to a wife he adored—he kept his nose clean and was never known for any destructive behavior. I only wished that the other ball players in my life were like him.

"Prepared to play the best game of your lives tonight?" I stopped, nailing them with my eyes so they knew I meant business.

"Sure thing, hot stuff." The player winked. I groaned inwardly just as my eyes landed on a soft, sympathetic gaze caressing mine.

"Show the woman some respect, asshole." Cash socked him in the shoulder, then turned. His eyes nailed mine, and I felt my lungs empty like rapidly deflating balloons. I still didn't know how I managed to keep my wits about me yesterday. Then last night while in bed, his dancing dark brown eyes and his cocky mouth ran through my head, the image so vivid that for a few moments I thought I could reach out and touch him.

The things Cash Greenwood made me feel didn't at all sit well with me. He was arrogant, conceited, and without a doubt a total manwhore, just like all the other players on the team. I remembered the headlines when his buddy Rodriguez had been caught getting lucky with a fan in the locker room a few years ago. That was a shitstorm, and so was he. And considering they say like attracts like, I was pretty sure Cash enjoyed the same excesses. He was just lucky that his escapades were yet to be caught on camera.

"Mornin'." Cash's body pressed up against mine, his fingers trailing across the skin at my wrist like a kiss. His kiss. What would Cash's kisses feel like? I could just imagine my fingers tracking along that rugged jawline, his broad palms splayed across my back when he pressed his lips to mine. I quickly snapped out of my reverie.

"All right, Ms. Grey?" Cash breathed against my neck and sent an explosion of flames through every last nerve ending I possessed. His breath was warm and tempting, almost intoxicating in its allure.

"I'm fine, thank you." I swallowed, taking a single step back and averting my eyes from his. "And good morning, Mr. Greenwood."

"Enjoy the game?" His lips hovered just inches from mine, close enough to send waves of arousal pounding through my blood.

"I told you, I don't like—"

"I know, I know, but I'm hoping I can change your mind about that."

"Doubt it. I've spent too many hours of my life in the dugout. I know what to expect, and it's not for me."

"Spent a lot of time in the dugout, huh?" He tipped his head to the side, narrowing his eyes as he worked over my words.

"Grew up in one."

He arched an eyebrow. "So…you must have someone in the family who played ball?"

"Maybe." I grinned, turning on my heel and retreating down the long hall that led to the field. I hadn't meant to reveal that bit of information about growing up in a ball field, but that doesn't mean I had to reveal anything else. I never told anyone about my childhood. The chaos that surrounded it was already too much for me to bear. I wasn't interested in rehashing any of it.

"Delilah!" Cash called, but I kept walking, pretending I couldn't hear. *Don't let him see you sweat, because if you turn around right now he's going to see the cheesy smile on your traitorous face.* I turned the corner, stepping up into the rows of seats and taking my place next to the dugout. I didn't like to be right in there with them, interrupting their flow, but I did like to be close throughout the game to get a sense of the players, learn their habits under pressure, and make a note of how they held themselves when cameras were on and thousands of pairs of eyes were watching their every move.

I watched as the players filtered out onto the field one by one, tossing balls and swinging bats as they warmed up. I may not have liked the jocks under those uniforms, but something about a ball field made me feel more at home than anything else ever had. The smell of the popcorn, the glare of the stadium lights, the sound of cleats on dusty bags as players rounded bases. I had a love-hate relationship with this game, I had been introduced to it at an early age and since then it had been a constant in my life. Dad had hauled me and my little sister to the ball field every time he played a home game in the summer. We'd bring our toys, books, anything we could think of to keep us busy as he played. I looked at the bench, then at the field, and happy memories as a little girl flooded me. Then, just like I had been hit by a hammer, the pain catapulted into my heart and mind. I quickly remembered why ball players were men that I needed to stay far away from.

"Jesus, where's Cash?" Coach hollered just as Cash came around the corner and jogged out onto the field, his walk-up song, "Greenlight" by Pitbull, pounding through the speakers. *Red light, green light, give me everything you got, red light, green light…*

Dammit, why did he have to be so tall and broad

and…sexy?

I averted my eyes to my phone, tapping out a text to meet a girlfriend for drinks later. I'd have to keep my mind preoccupied if I was going to spend every day of the next nine months watching him play.

Any hot players you can hook me up with? Tori replied.

I groaned.

Why did it seem like the universe was conspiring against me?

Ball players suck, Tori. ;)

I waited for her answer, my eyes lifting and catching Cash's gaze on mine. What the hell? Why was he looking at me? A crooked grin turned his lips before he brushed his thumb across his lower lip.

His really full lower lip.

I frowned, turning back to my phone to find Tori had replied.

Gimme names. I'll Google them and tell you which ones are bangable.

I choked down a laugh before typing out. *I'm working! You're being a distraction!*

Isn't that what you wanted, a distraction? Came her quick reply.

Yes, but I don't think of these guys like that. I have a job to do. I waited, ready to shove the phone in my bag and ignore her altogether.

Then why aren't you doing it instead of texting me? ;)

I sent her the middle finger emoji, then dropped the phone into my bag and turned my eyes back to the players. Cash was waiting near the dugout, swinging a bat as he waited for his turn at bat. His gaze swung across the crowd, settling on mine instantly.

He stared intently, as if he wanted to speak to me without words, before he finally tipped his helmet and stood straight. He was well over six feet, the uniform hanging perfectly on his body, in just the right way to hint at the taut muscles beneath. I shifted in my seat, feeling an unfamiliar throbbing between my thighs. I'd never been turned on by a guy in uniform before. What the hell was going on with me? Was this some sort of premature midlife crisis? I'd vowed over and over again to never even look at a baseball player. Like breaking a bad habit, I'd trained my mind to divert whenever I saw an attractive one, but it wasn't working this time. Cash was on my mind all the time.

"Damn you, Cash Greenwood," I said out loud, knowing he wouldn't be able to make out my words from all the way across the field. I had to stay professional, keep my wits about me. *Don't let him get under your skin, Delilah.*

Cash grinned at me one last time before turning his attention to the pitcher and slamming a wild home run right out of the ball park. My eyes widened at the sheer force of his batting abilities. No wonder he was on the radar of every single team in Major League Baseball. The man was a monster, a force to be reckoned with. This was going to be a long day. Him, his pitching and catching, and me, tamping down my urge to rip his clothes off.

I knew sitting here for the next three hours would be torture. Because every time I glanced up, my eyes somehow found his, like we were in the middle of a magnetic field. I hated that magnetic field. It was complete and utter bullshit.

Nearly four hours later, when I'd finally packed up my laptop and headed out of the stands and down into the inside of the stadium, I took the long, dark back hallway to the employee parking area. I hadn't spoken to any of the players after the game. I'd promised Coach the stats by morning, so there was no chance I could stop and get that drink with Tori.

I dug through the oversized bag on my shoulder, pulling out my phone to text her, when I ran smack into a wall of a body. "Jesus, I'm sorry."

"If you wanted to touch me, Grey, you could have just asked." Cash. Dammit.

"Hardly." I narrowed my eyes. I knew there was no logical reason for my distaste toward him, but my history with ball players and my attraction to him made me insane. It was a lethal combination of hate and lust. Besides, I had no patience for arrogance, and it came off of him in waves. Sexy waves of bulging muscle, rich eyes, and the face of a rugged angel. Why did he have to be so damn attractive?

"In a hurry? Let's get a drink."

"No can do, Greenwood. I've got stats to run tonight."

"Sounds fun. I'll bring pizza."

My eyes nearly popped out of my head. "No, I need to focus. You are the last thing I want in my life."

"Or exactly the thing you didn't know you needed."

"Are you always so…"

"Charming?" His lips twitched up in a smile.

"I was going to say *irritating*." His grin turned wider then, and I swear to God, my ovaries just exploded while my heart skipped a beat.

"I'll warn you, I don't have any plans of giving up anytime soon." His presence ate up all the oxygen between us. It had to be a hundred degrees in this hallway. I placed a hand to my neck, my mind racing with the effect he had. I wondered if I looked like how I felt, desperate, needy, and a little confused. That combination was one that caused anger to simmer within me. I just wanted to get away, but something was keeping me at a standstill.

"Why not? I've made it clear you and I are never happening."

"Because you're the only woman who's ever made me interested enough to try before. That makes you and me a sure thing."

"What?" I laughed. "That's some twisted logic, Cash."

"See, I made you laugh. You need more people in your life who make you laugh."

"How on earth would you know what I need more of in my life?"

"I can see it in your eyes—focused, driven, a little lonely." His thumb slid down the line of my neck. Just the faintest of touches, sending a wildfire blazing through my body.

"You're wrong on one of those three."

"Yeah," He leaned a little closer, his soapy, post-shower skin like a powerful punch to my girl parts. "I guess you weren't so focused earlier."

His thumb danced across the curve of my jaw. I clenched my fists, vibrating with some sort of heady arousal I'd never felt before. "Good night, Greenwood."

"Cash. Call me Cash! I liked hearing the sound of my name on the sweetest lips I've ever seen," he called, but I was already halfway down the hall, the sound of my heels echoing through my ears. "Good night, Delilah!" I heard his soft chuckle, turning only once as I pushed through the doors to chance a final glance his way.

He was still standing there, hands on hips, and the most amused smile I'd ever seen on his sexy lips.

I had never really been a fan of my name. It always seemed bland and rather boring, so why had it felt like fireworks blasting off in my stomach when he did it?

Damn that arrogant son of a bitch and his pretty smile.

3

Cash

"Mornin', Delilah." I grinned, enjoying the way her lips twitched when I passed her the hot cup of coffee.

"You got that for me?" She crooked one eyebrow. Damn, she was beautiful. My stomach flipped wildly with just that one look. I didn't know what she was doing to me, but I definitely wanted her, and I had never wanted another before her.

"Just for you."

Delilah glanced around the meeting room, her eyes making contact with a few of the other players that were watching our exchange. "Thank you."

She took the coffee cautiously, pursing her lips just

slightly as she took her first sip.

"My pleasure." My gaze lingered, eyes traveling across her gorgeous face, the way her mouth lifted in a smirk, the way her eyes danced like she had so much to say she could barely contain it.

But contain it she did. Delilah was the most reserved woman I'd ever met, but that just made me want to know more about her. I'd gone to bed last night with Delilah on my mind, and although I was amused by her constant rebuffs, I'd decided to take things up a notch. Delilah was special, I knew it down in my bones, and I was going to show her that she needed to give me a shot. I was determined to do anything to win this girl, absolutely anything. I'd have to dig deep for it given that I spent my days around a group of macho jocks. Of course, I could be a little rough around the edges, but I had a feeling all of our edges would fit just fine when it finally happened. I just had to show her.

"Let's go out to dinner sometime." I lowered my voice, holding her captive with my gaze. Her eyes were so captivating, I was transported. I couldn't believe that just staring into her eyes would make me so damn happy. I felt like a fool, but this was so new to me. My whole life I'd never thought that I would meet a girl like her, yet here she was looking at me, piercing me, making me feel things in all the dark places in my soul. I'd been drowning for thirty years, baseball my only lifeline, and now here was this stunning woman who made me want things, things I probably didn't have any business wanting, but I fucking wanted them. And I wanted them with her.

She sucked in a breath, setting the coffee on the table next to her before she shook her head. "You don't take no for an answer, do you?"

"No isn't my thing, I prefer positive thinking. You know, when first you don't succeed, dust yourself off and try again."

She chuckled before running a hand through her hair. She'd worn it down today. Goddamn, she'd worn it down and it curled over one shoulder and caressed all her soft curves. My mouth watered, actually watered, begging to get a taste.

Fuck, I wanted to be against a wall, tasting her with my tongue, hearing her moans crash down on my ears.

"You're cute, Cash, I'll give you that. But that's it. Dating a ball player isn't my thing. Let's just say I have an aversion to them."

"I don't believe that for a second," I said.

"Well, I'm telling you, it's true."

"I know you keep saying you hate ball players, but I think there is something else. You didn't have to take this job, Delilah."

She frowned, her eyes narrowing on me, swirling with fire and passion and everything that made my dick pound so fucking hard behind my zipper I thought I might lose my fucking mind. "Baseball players are ignorant pigs, but they lead the industry in analytics, so here I am."

"You're sweet when you get all fired up."

"Cash!" She huffed, turning back to the coffee at the table and thrusting it at me. "If accepting this coffee means we have to be friends, you can have it back."

I laughed, following her out the doors and into the hallway, away from all the guys. "What is your favorite type of food?"

"What? No, Cash. I mean it. I think you're disgusting,

and I promise there will never be one thing between us."

I turned, my gaze focused on hers. "Then why does your breathing pick up whenever I come in the room? And why couldn't you keep your eyes off me during the game? Lie to yourself all you want, Delilah." I leaned in, twisting a soft lock of hair through my fingers. "But you can't lie to me. You feel it, too."

She paused, her jaw tight as her labored pants grew even more frantic. "You're infuriating, Cash Greenwood. And don't forget, if you piss me off I can fudge your numbers." She crossed her arms adorably, but it only served to push her gorgeous tits up even higher, drawing attention to the fact that she was full of curves and heaven-sent for a man like me. God, I had never seen anything so beautiful.

"But you won't."

She shook her head, and I swear I was waiting for her to stomp her foot with fury.

"You'd never compromise the job, because despite everything you say, you love being here." My mouth twisted in a smile as she puffed out a breath of air.

"Fine. You're right. But believe me, if I were an asshole it's the first thing I would do, Greenwood."

"Bullshit." I caught her chin between my fingers. "You're too good for that, and that's why I find you so damn irresistible. Beautiful beyond reason and stronger than I ever could have imagined. And that, my sweet Delilah, is why you are something I want in my universe. I'm a man who appreciates perfection, and you are perfect."

I spun and walked back into the room, sliding out a chair before dropping down into it to take a sip of my own coffee. Her eyes were still on me, shocked as she watched my every move. I smiled sweetly at her, loving the hell out of this game we were playing. But eventually she would be mine. I was one of the best players in Major League Baseball, and it wasn't just because I was gifted. It was because when I set my mind on a goal, I kept at it until I achieved it. And Delilah was worth more than any other goal I had ever had in my entire life.

Delilah shook her head, finally breaking my gaze and turning her attention to the players filtering into the room to prepare for the analytics meeting.

Delilah had only been here less than a few days and already the energy in the locker room was different. The guys a little more respectful, all except Rod, of course, and Coach seemed to be digging all the new stats that Delilah could provide after every play.

She was brilliant, she was pretty, she was sexy, and she was fierce. I tapped my fingers on the desk as Delilah cleared her voice and started the meeting.

"Numbers were good last night. Great job, you guys. We can talk individually about a few things each of you should work on, but so far the numbers look even better than last year. Carlos, you threw 96 on that pitch last night. That was stellar."

The team clapped before Delilah continued. "And that home run was your best yet, Miller." She turned to another teammate and gave him a wide smile. What the fuck? I'd hit four homers during the game—where were my stats? I shifted in my seat, clearing my throat before Delilah's eyes glanced to me, then away again, her eyes shifting down to her laptop as she rattled off a few more numbers and congratulated the team members.

"Unless Coach has any questions, I think we're done, then."

"I've got a question," I spoke up.

Delilah's eyes didn't meet my gaze. Damn, she was baiting me. She hadn't wanted to draw attention to us, so she was avoiding my ass altogether. But I was the star pitcher. I needed my stats if I was going to have any idea how I'd played. I'd felt strong, powerful, smooth, and efficient, but the numbers helped confirm that in my head.

"What's up, Cash?" Coach chimed in when he saw Delilah wasn't answering.

"Well, considering I pitched four innings last night, I'd like to know my stats."

Delilah narrowed her eyes, sending daggers at me before she made a few clicks on her laptop, then twisted it around for me to see. "Your numbers are down."

"What? How is that possible? I pitched a great game."

She shrugged, spinning the laptop to her again. I couldn't believe I hadn't been on top of it last night. My mind rattled with anxiety as I wondered if turning 30 also meant my career was headed down the toilet. A lot of guys didn't make it to forty in this business, I knew that, but I'd hoped with constant and focused practice I could beat the odds, at least for a while. If I was looking at retirement anytime soon, I might lose my mind.

"It's normal for players to take a few games to get into the swing of things and see the numbers they were seeing end of last season."

I frowned deeper, taking another long drink of my coffee, my muscles bunched and tensed as I thought I needed to get into the bullpen and throw a few more balls a few more hours every day. I knew pitchers were the first to show signs of age, shoulder injuries the most common problem, but damn if I was going to let that happen to me.

Suddenly feeling like I couldn't be in the room any longer, I stood, scraping the chair loudly across the floor before leaving the room, the door closing with a resounding thump.

4

Delilah

I walked down the long corridor, my heels echoing on the cement floors as I headed for the coach's office to leave the reports I'd printed for the players' stats. The repetitive *thud thud thud* of a baseball hitting workout pads took me back to a time when I was so much younger, so much more impressionable, so much more out of control than I was now.

I paused when I reached the semi-soundproof room, my eyes widening when I realized Cash was the one throwing balls on repeat. The meeting had ended an hour and a half ago—had he been here the whole time, practicing until he blew his arm out for tonight's game? I frowned, leaning against the door as I watched him. He was determined, hell-bent on getting his arm stronger, and focused like I'd never seen in all my years of watching this sport. His arm wound up, and with the force of an oncoming truck, he launched the little white ball across the room. *Thwack!*

I sighed, my eyes taking in the lean lines of his chiseled body. He was hands-down the hottest guy on the team, and his ass in a pair of baseball pants was one of the biggest distractions I faced on this job. If I wasn't gritting my teeth when he cast me that sexy, one-sided smile, I was squirming in my seat checking him out from behind.

It was like an uncontrollable primal impulse. If Cash was in the room, my body was on high alert.

Cash finally paused, working his arm back and forth and rubbing at it with a wince.

"Shit," I murmured before opening the door and letting myself in. "Don't wear your arm out, Cash."

His eyes flashed up with surprise, his face softening for a minute when he saw me. He shook his head. "I don't do second best, and your numbers from last night indicate that, so I'm going to work like hell until my pitch is what it was last year."

I paused the thoughts rushing through my brain as, for once, I saw the thing that he really cared about, the thing that lit fire in his eyes and made him more determined than ever. I respected that in him.

"You'll get there."

He shook his head again, still rubbing at his shoulder as he looked down at his feet. "If I don't have baseball, I don't have anything. I have to get there or it's the beginning of the end for me."

"Cash…" My heart bled for him. I walked behind him and rubbed at the tight knot forming in his shoulder. "Don't be so hard on yourself."

He didn't say anything, but his muscles began to relax as I kneaded at the tight tissue. I licked my lips, sucking in a breath of air for the first time since I'd stepped into his presence. I caught a whiff of his woodsy scent, soap, and the pure mix of him, and it left me dizzy with arousal.

"You're going to have to see the massage therapist for this arm before the game." I used both my hands to work at his shoulder and down his bicep.

Good lord, his arms were so massive. The way the fabric pulled across the expanse of his strong shoulders was the sexiest thing I'd ever seen. An unbidden fantasy slipped into my thoughts—me, wearing his jersey and not another stitch of clothing.

Oh my God, where had that come from? I didn't do this, didn't fraternize with players, didn't mix business with pleasure. God, I didn't date ball players! For that matter, I didn't even date, as sad and pathetic as that was. My hands dropped instantly, all the old triggers bubbling up and making me want to run from the room, and from Cash, as quickly as humanly possible.

"Thanks for the pep talk." Cash turned then, his eyes leveling with mine as silence stretched between us.

"Thank you for the coffee this morning." I finally interrupted the silence. "It was nice of you."

"I can be a pretty nice guy. I wish you'd give me a chance to show you."

A small grin lifted my mouth before I shook my head. "Persistent must be your middle name."

"Delilah," His hands were at my shoulders, his body pushing both of us against the padded walls of the workout room. "I promise, whoever gave you the bad impression of ball players, I'm not them." His nose snaked along my neck and sent shivers coursing in molten waves through my veins.

I slammed my eyes closed, sucking in vital breaths of oxygen even though he was too close, he was right here, his lips inches away from being pressed against mine.

"I want to taste those pretty lips." Cash's voice ate up the air between us. My mind raged, my stomach flipped, fire burned from my toes all the way to my head. "And that look on your face tells me you need kissing, and I know I'm the only man to do it."

My hands slipped up his chest, the hard ridges of muscle sending tingles like fireworks through my fingers. I didn't know what this was, but it felt like waves of energy coming off him, melding with mine, syncing together and bonding us inexplicably. I was drunk on Cash Greenwood, just like every other girl who sat in those bleachers or watched him play a game on TV.

I couldn't deal with those other girls.

This life wasn't for me. I was sure of that, at least.

"Cash, we're not going to happen. Thank you for the coffee, I hope your shoulder starts feeling better, but please don't make this harder than it has to be."

"What's hard about it, Delilah? You're the first woman I've ever seen in my life who makes me feel things a man feels for a woman. Fuck your stereotypes and look at me, not the game. I've never fucked a baseball groupie. My head's in the game and that's it. I've never loved anything more than I love baseball, but damn, you make me want to love you. Delilah, you walk into a room and you're all I see. In that stadium of 60,000 people, it's you I see. When I close my eyes at night, it's your face I dream of." His thumb trailed across my lower lip, causing it to tremble and me to melt under his touch. "And I know you see me, too."

I sucked in desperate breaths, willing my brain to work, willing my body to run, to scream, to kiss, to anything. Anything. Move, Delilah. Tell him to stop touching you, Delilah.

But I couldn't. I was rooted in place.

"You're not ready, but you'll get there. We make sense, Delilah. You just need to stop denying it and see it for what it really is."

I shook my head, fighting angry tears that had climbed up the back of my throat. I knew he was right. I knew I'd built a wall around my heart. It was all out of protection. I didn't want to be scared and alone again.

"You're wrong, Cash. You couldn't be more wrong." I dropped my palms from his chest and turned for the door, the lie tainting my lips like poison.

I curled up on the couch, wearing snowflake PJs and a tank top, with a blanket wrapped around my legs as I watched the game that night. I usually liked to be present. I'd found that chatting with the coach during the game often helped him make decisions about who to put in next, especially when I had the ability to run stats on the other team, but I could work from home almost as easily. I was determined and dedicated, but Cash had thrown me a curveball this afternoon.

His hands on my skin...his breath whispering across my neck were like a ghost haunting my memories. I pressed a hand to my chest, the memory so powerful a wild shiver raced through me. In all the teams I'd done consulting with, never had I had this issue, but I'd also never worked with a baseball team before, either. Maybe that was my problem. Maybe I should have steered clear knowing it was a trigger of mine.

Or maybe it was just Cash Greenwood.

I sighed, watching the seventh inning. Pitbull's *Greenlight* blasted through the stadium and pumped up the crowd as Cash walked to home plate. Conflicting emotions steamrolled through my mind as I watched him. He was thoughtful, smart, so incredibly sexy it was dangerous, and quite possibly the most talented human being I'd ever known. And that said a lot given I'd met a lot of talented players over the years.

Cash bent his knees, his eyes intent on the pitcher before the ball flew to home plate and Cash swung, a crack splitting the cool night air as the ball went high. I watched riveted as he launched for first base, his eyes on the ball as it sliced through the outfield, finally landing just out of reach of the outfielder on the other team.

He'd gotten to second.

Good, okay. He didn't look too bad, his shoulder didn't seem to bother him at all. I didn't know it'd light a fire under him when I'd told him his numbers were down, but he'd surprised the hell out of me with his focus, to the point that it concerned me. Practice was a fine balance between honing your skills and overdoing it. Fatigued muscles didn't play good baseball, but Cash seemed okay.

I watched as another batter took the plate, a shortstop whom I hadn't had much interaction with yet, but he hit a grounder to right field, and Cash launched off the bag again, headed for third. His eyes were focused as his legs powered him across the field, carrying him to third while the batter landed on first.

One more hit and Cash was home. Another point to break ahead in this game. They'd been tied since the third inning, and it was beginning to feel like this game would go into extra innings, until Cash had batted anyway.

Rodriguez stepped up to the plate before the other team waved their pitcher in and replaced him with another. Their star pitcher. Shit.

I tapped out a quick text to the manager of the team, knowing he'd be the only one to see my text since Coach was always so focused on what was happening on the field.

Jones throws a killer curveball. Tell Rodriguez to move about two inches away from the plate and he'll shatter it.

I was relieved when the manager's text shot back a second later. ***Thanks.***

I was doubly relieved when I caught a signal from one of the guys on the bench, catching Rodriguez's eyes and flashing him the sign for curveball. Rodriguez nodded, took half a step back from the plate, then assumed the position. All eyes were on him. With two outs he had to nail this one if we were going to pull ahead.

I watched Cash, his body fluid and strong like the well-honed machine he was. Never in my life had I been so turned on, and I couldn't even bring myself to care anymore. Sitting in front of this TV watching the game, I felt safer, more protected, more willing to indulge my teen-girl fantasies of shagging the hottest player on the team. I couldn't bring myself to flirt with him in the flesh, but right here on my couch, fantasies were running wild.

The pitcher wound up his arm, eyes flashing as he released the ball, and just like I'd predicted, that ball curved deeply to the left before approaching home plate. Rodriguez's body tensed, his fists white as he clutched the bat. He powered through his swing and sent the ball flying far out into left field, way beyond Cash, far beyond their outfielder, until it ricocheted right off the wall of the outfield, bouncing onto the turf as Cash and Miller launched from their bases. Like a well-oiled machine, each player rounded the field while the outfielder finally grabbed the ball and launched it to the pitcher, hoping to get it home before Cash could score.

I shrieked, jumping up in my small living room and clapping just as Cash's foot landed on home. Safe.

Suddenly I was sad that I wasn't there in person to celebrate with the team. The energy of the crowd pulsed through you, energizing you and raising the stakes of the game. I loved being at the field more than I'd even realized.

I sat back down on the couch when the team high-fived Cash in the dugout, a broad smile lighting his face. He was devastatingly handsome. He laughed with the guys and nodded his head as he cheered the other players on when it was their turn. I was completely enamored with him, and I hated every minute.

I hated that he was, in fact, sweet. He'd pulled at my heartstrings earlier today when he'd touched me, because that sent my body into a danger zone. It terrified me, all the painful memories of my past coming to the surface as my heart and my head fought for dominance.

Cash made me crazy, but I was beginning to find

myself addicted to that feeling down low in my stomach.

The truth was, I'd never felt this way about anyone, either. I'd always been a pro at turning off my feelings and ruling with my head, statistics and numbers filling the empty spaces most people packed with love and sex and money.

Watching Cash play was equal parts maddening and thrilling, and part of me thought if I had to watch anyone play baseball for the rest of my life, I'd choose him.

5

Cash

I shoved a hand through my damp hair, a bag of my favorite noodle takeout in hand. It was late, the game had ended less than an hour ago, and all I could think about doing was seeing her, talking about the game with her, just talking to her.

"Hello?" The door swung open, and her pretty lips dropped into an O.

"Evenin'."

"Cash, what are you—"

"I brought food." I lifted the bag in my hand. "From the noodle shop next to my house."

A stubborn grin lifted her features, and I thought right then and there I was done for. I was cracking her tough shell and that thought alone nearly killed me in the best way.

"I like noodles." She opened the door wider. "You're spoiling me. When someone else turns your head and you finally give up on me, I'm going to miss the gestures."

"Well, obviously you don't know me well enough yet." I stepped into her living room, my eyes holding hers. "Because I don't give up."

Her eyes held mine for a long beat before she slowly nodded. "I'm learning that."

She snagged the bag from my hands and turned, and for the first time my eyes cast down her curvy body. She wore the cutest goddamn pair of snowflake pajamas I'd ever seen, made all the more endearing by the fact that it wasn't even winter. The thin straps of her tank top begged for my teeth and made me want to peel the clothing off her body one inch at a time and track my tongue up and down all her luscious curves.

She reached the kitchen and turned, pulling plates from the cupboard before opening up the brown bag. She leaned over, pulling forks from a drawer, the deep vee of her cleavage making my cock throb painfully behind the zipper of my jeans. I'd never so blatantly checked out a woman before—I had respect for the female population—but there was something about Delilah that turned me into a raging caveman myself.

I licked my lips, wondering what her nipples would taste like on my tongue, the faint outline of those little tight buds peeking through the cotton and causing my brain to flood with a thousand fantasies, all starring her.

"Did you watch the game?" I took a plate from her hand as she gestured for me to sit on the couch with her. She must have been snuggled up in blankets all night, working from the couch with her laptop. I see a long spreadsheet of numbers filling the screen.

"Of course." She took a bite of her noodles, then moaned. "These are the best noodles I've *everrrrr* had." My dick jumped at the soft noise escaping her pretty lips. How I longed to make her moan like that as my tongue roamed her luscious body. What was it about this girl that made me so damn crazy?

Because she's the most beautiful thing you've ever seen.

I sighed, averting my eyes to the TV, where she had ESPN playing on low volume, updates from all the MLB games scrolling along the bottom feed.

Christ, she watched the sports channel, too. Could she be anymore perfect?

"You've been working all night?"

"Mhmm." She hummed as she ate.

"You know you could probably take some of that advice you dished out early about pushing yourself too hard."

"No, it's totally different for me." She shook her head and twirled her fork in the pile of noodles.

"Hardly."

"Definitely." She narrowed her eyes for a moment, but I saw the amused grin tipping her lips. "How did you find out where I live, anyway?"

I shrugged. "A determined man has his ways."

"So you're a stalker?"

"Only if you like being stalked, baby. I can be anything you want me to be."

"You're impossible." She turned up the volume on the

TV, attempting to cut off this conversation.

I turned it right back down on her. "Coach gave me your phone number, I did a reverse lookup and got lucky. Did you know you're listed for any stranger to see online?"

"Aren't we all?"

"Yeah, but that's dangerous for a single woman. Maybe you should get a dog or something."

"Seems like I've got my own right now."

I laughed at her insinuation that I was a dog. That was so far from the truth. If only she knew.

"So what brings you by, other than the noodles? Thank you, by the way."

"I just wanted to see if you were okay. After earlier...I just wanted to say...well." I shoved a hand through my hair. "I'm not sure what I wanted to say except that I missed you at the game. You know, I had a hard time concentrating when I didn't see you. So I wanted to see you and make sure you were okay. And feed you. I'm afraid you don't eat."

The chuckle that echoed around the space was like a siren song to my battered heart. "I eat plenty, but the noodles are delicious. If it weren't for them, I would have kicked you out already by now."

"I believe it. You're a tiger, Delilah."

She paused, her eyes glazing with some inexplicable emotion before she turned back to the TV, taking another bite from her plate.

"What was that? What did I say?"

"I just..." She pursed her lips as she thought. "I don't talk about myself much, so this is hard for me, but you've got to understand something, Cash. You're sweet, you really are—"

53

"And handsome."

She giggled. "Yeah, a little. But this still isn't going to happen between us. And I have a feeling the only reason you want me is because I'm the only girl who doesn't fall all over you when you walk into a room."

"That's not true for a second." I set my plate down and inched across the couch to her. "Your smile drives me insane, the way your lips curve up just right here…" I dusted my thumb across the corner of her mouth. "It undoes me. The way your eyes light up when you're passionate about something, which is pretty much everything—"

"Cash?" My name whispers past her delicate lips.

"Yeah, baby."

"You have to stop touching me."

I dropped my hand instantly, eyes narrowing. Her gaze caught mine before she shrank away. "You don't know what you're getting into."

"Tell me then."

"No, no, let's just keep this professional."

"I don't know if I can do that."

"Why, Cash? I'm just a girl. There's nothing special about me. I'm nerdy and quiet and way too cerebral. I live alone and I like it. Relationships just aren't for me."

I shook my head, listening to her explain but not believing a damn word of it. "You should see yourself the way I see you."

Her eyes widened as her chest rose and fell with her breaths. "And how's that?"

"Intoxicating. Dizzying. Completely fucking incredible in every way."

"You're crazy and delusional."

I shook my head, a smile pulling at my lips as I

watched her in the dim light of the living room. "Or maybe I'm drunk on you."

She set her plate down, glancing at the clock on the screen before swallowing and turning back to me. "Cash...you don't understand what I've been through. I've been around ball players my entire life. I remember my dad coming home from practice reeking of booze and women, and starting fights with my mom. It was horrible. One night I hid in my closet, all the stuffed animals I owned piled on top of me. I was convinced they'd keep me safe... The things my parents said to each other, no person should ever say to anyone they love. I'm not even sure they loved each other. It looked a whole lot more like hate to me. My mother would just sit there on the floor afterwards, crying or medicating herself to sleep, and my father would storm out, going out to look for more baseball groupies who would do whatever he said and never talk back or question him." The thought of her as a little girl, all alone and scared, ripped my heart out. No wonder she had such an aversion to ball players, it made perfect sense.

"You didn't deserve that, Delilah." I caught her hand in mine, heart aching for the little girl she'd been and for all the pain she still carried on her shoulders. I'd do anything to fix it for her. She deserved a life filled with love and happiness, and I wanted to be the man to give it to her. I loved baseball, but at some point that world would fade away. Delilah was forever. What we could have together would last an eternity. She was just too stubborn to see it, but I'd crack her shell. I already had.

"The baseball life isn't for me, Cash. I'll never be a woman who can be a ball player's wife—all the women, the partying, the late nights. I like boring, predictable, and stable. Those are the things that matter to me. So what if you give me a few butterflies—"

"I give you butterflies?" I teased.

"You give me a case of *wild* butterflies. So many butterflies I think I might be sick, so you see, you really make me sick to my stomach, which isn't a good thing," she finished, a satisfied smile on her gorgeous face.

"You know what I call that?" I leaned a little closer, soaking up her sexy scent as I whispered at her neck. "Chemistry. Anticipation. *Desire.*"

Delilah's pulse quickened at her neck, her body shifting as ragged little breaths parted her pouty little lips. "I'm a stubborn girl, Cash."

"I guarantee I'm a more determined man."

I could wait Delilah out. I was working the long game.

6

Delilah

A half a dozen games later, I sat in a quiet hotel room running statistics for the game we'd lost tonight. The team was better—the analytics I'd run before had proven it—but it didn't make the loss any less crushing. A few of the guys on the team were spending time in the hotel VIP bar drinking off their loss and preparing to face the same team tomorrow. The Timberwolves could do it. I knew they could. There was so much talent on this team, but we had to get the strategy straight, and that took a lot of time and a lot of analyzing, which was why I was plopped here in pajamas working at nearly midnight.

Cash and I hadn't spoken much since he'd come to my place with takeout, a move that had shocked the hell out of me, but made me feel good just the same. If anything, it was nice to have a friend, even if getting involved with him wasn't on my radar. I'd done my best all week to avoid his eyes, focusing instead on the game, and working hours and hours into the night just for the distraction.

The instant I shut my eyes, I found Cash lurking in my head, begging me to try just a taste. I didn't want a taste, dammit, and if anything, this job was proving why I didn't have time for it. I knew I could be an asset to this team, helping Coach make decisions based on the numbers we ran of all the teams in the Major League. I just had to stay focused. This was a big contract, and anything less than a stellar job would be a dent in the reputation of my company. I'd finally started making enough to hire a few statistics majors fresh out of college, and they were now stationed at a few clubs around the country. We were making a good name for ourselves, as long as we continued our hot streak.

I had a feeling the Timberwolves could win the pennant this year, and if I analyzed their performances right, maybe even the World Series.

I stood up to pour another glass of cheap wine from the mini-bar when a soft knock came from the door. My eyes shot up, wondering who on earth would be knocking at this hour. Probably one of the drunk team members. Coach had told them to go light tonight, but losing a game hurt, and a lot of them liked to drown their frustration in booze.

I cracked the door, ever cautious because being on the wrong side of a drunk ball player was never my idea of a good time, when I saw Cash's dark eyes peering back at me.

"What's wrong?" I swung the door wide, and he stepped in.

He shook his head, only gazing at me. I could see the disappointment lacing his features. He was more upset at the loss than the rest of the guys. His dedication and complete disappointment over this loss were a testament to just how much he loved this game, and how much he expected of himself. I had no doubt he gave two hundred percent every game, but sometimes even that wasn't enough. "I don't know what happened."

"Cash…" I sighed, closing the door behind him and heading back to the mini-bar. "Bad games happen, that's all. Road games are never easy."

I turned when he didn't answer and saw his eyes burning up the space between us with something I couldn't quite place.

"Really fucking glad you're here, Delilah." He moved toward me, his hands at my jawline before his lips were pressed to mine. I opened up, and our tongues tangled together as fire burned its way up from my toes and down through my torso to land in a delicious wave of arousal between my thighs.

I pushed my hands into his hair as his palms cupped my ass cheeks, then he hoisted me in his strong arms and pushed us both against the wall. His body between my thighs was rock solid and heated with all the emotion pulsing through his system. "I don't know what the hell you're doing to me."

I didn't answer, only attacking his lips with more fevered thrusts, my hips rocking against him as I sought any kind of friction to relieve the ache he'd created. One of his palms trailed up under the silk of my cami, his fingers dancing across my skin and leaving a white-hot blaze in their path.

I knew he'd tried to express respect for me this past week by steering clear. Apparently he'd recognized that I needed it, but if anything, the separation had only fueled the obsession.

We kissed for long minutes, hands and breath washing across skin and sending my system into lust-filled overload.

"I think you were put here to drive me insane." He hummed, his tongue tracing up the line of my neck as his hands pushed at the straps of my cami.

"We're all wrong for each other."

"I don't think so."

"I can't stand you," I gasped when his hand slid between my thighs and pressed at my damp pussy through the fabric of my shorts. "But I can't stand to be away from you, either."

He groaned. "Christ, me neither, beautiful. I've been waiting for those words."

"Cash…" I moaned as his thumb swirled, pressing and massaging at the hardened bud that would send me into a state of bliss.

"Fuck, I need you." His thumb sped up, and my thighs began to tighten and quiver around his hips. "It kills me to see you walking around in those fuck-me heels, that tight skirt that shows off every curve you have. All I can think about is getting under it, tasting your sweet cunt until you scream." His lips caressed my ear. "I don't like other people seeing what's mine, Delilah."

My breathing picked up, and my head fell back against the wall, and just when his touch felt like too much, like I might explode from the inside out, waves of frantic pleasure careened through my body. Moans fell past my lips before I tried to clamp down on my teeth to suppress them.

"Let them hear you, sweetheart. I want every goddamn man in this hotel to know you're off limits. You are mine, only mine, from now until forever. I want you in the worst way, your scent, your touch, your smile, your everything. I want your face to be the last thing I see at night and the first thing I see in the morning. I want to mark you, and I want you to mark me. This is it, Delilah. This is our forever. "

"But Cash…"

"I want you, Delilah, I want everything you have to give, and I'll get it."

"No, but—"

"Shhh," he hissed before plunging his tongue past my lips, tasting me like he was starved for every last drop. Both of his hands circled my neck, his thumbs caressing the sensitive skin beneath my ears as he kissed me. God, I loved how he held my head when we kissed. I hated that I loved every minute of it. Hated that it was him who turned me on. Hated that I was falling for a ball player. But falling for Cash Greenwood was what I was doing. I was falling fast and hard, and in my heart I knew there was nothing I could do about it. It was a hunger that was insatiable and a passion that burned hotter than fire.

But deep down that little girl was too scared, too weak to take a chance. My parents broke me somehow, and as much as I wanted Cash, as much as I was falling for him, that little girl was screaming for me to stop.

"Cash?" I finally whispered when I'd taken a breath,

our lungs gasping for air we didn't have. He pressed his forehead to mine, his heart thrumming frantically against mine as we paused in the darkened room and soaked up the passion-fueled mess we'd found ourselves in. "We can't do this."

Cash didn't reply, his fingertips hovering across my skin before he finally placed his lips to mine in one last kiss. His hands dropped from my skin, and he took two steps back, lowering my feet to the floor.

He pushed a hand through his tousled hair, his eyes squeezed shut while he scrubbed a palm over his face. He was fucked up, not from booze, not even from me, from this game.

"I'm sorry," I offered lamely, thinking this hadn't been the right time, but his tongue down my throat hadn't exactly been foreseen either.

"Why? Why fight this? I know you feel it, Grey. I know that every fiber of your being wants me as much as I want you. We are perfect for each other, and I have a hard time believing that the first woman I want isn't the one."

My eyes widened at his words, my heart kicking into high gear. His eyes were on me now, waiting for my reply.

"Because...I..." I had no words. Cash left me at a loss for words, and suddenly the ones I'd been saying in my head seemed all wrong. "My past, it's just...I have triggers."

His eyes narrowed. "That's bullshit. We all have triggers. My whole life, something was missing. Thirty damn years and something was off. I thought it was my rocky childhood, my single-minded love of the game, but it wasn't. It was you, Delilah. My whole damn life I was searching for you. I know you want me. I can see it in your eyes, the way your gaze follows me across the room."

"I never meant to send mixed signals…" I trailed off, knowing my words were zero consolation. I was a girl with a ton of emotional triggers—well-founded, if you asked me—but that didn't mean I could just shake them off in favor of giving him what he wanted. In fact, that was the last thing that was going to happen. "I also have a job today. Getting involved with one of you—"

"I'm not just one of those guys. I'm not a fucking manwhore that sleeps with everything. I've never slept with a woman, Delilah. I'm a goddamn virgin." His anger was rising, his cheeks reddening as he became more animated.

"Don't bullshit me, Cash. A thirty-year-old star pitcher, hitter, and virgin? I don't buy it."

His eyes cast down, his lip caught between his teeth, and he turned, waltzing straight out of my room, not sparing me a single glance back. With one resounding bang of the heavy door, he was gone and I was alone, wondering what in the hell I'd done to find myself here.

I touched my lips, still tingling from his kiss, feeling bruised from his lips pressed to mine. Sweet God, that kiss had been otherworldly. And how could I ever kiss anyone else again? No one could live up to Cash.

My situation felt impossible, so I turned back to the bar, poured my glass of wine, then went back to the bed and my laptop. I took a sip and thought about returning to the numbers tonight, but my focus wasn't there. Cash had shattered it. Cash's lips had shattered me.

I sighed, slamming my laptop closed and reclining back in the bed. I flicked on ESPN to get the latest game highlights, but pitifully, the only topic of conversation was the Timberwolves and their uncharacteristic and blatantly bad loss. I nearly flicked off when one announcer spoke up, pausing on a clip of Rodriguez stumbling the first time he went up to bat. They were speculating he was drunk and perhaps that contributed to the lost game. He'd had a few strikeouts and had missed more than a few catches that he should have caught.

My heart fell between my feet.

Fucking Rodriguez.

7

Cash

I jogged out onto the field the next morning, my muscles threaded with adrenaline. Delilah had consumed all my thoughts last night—the memory of her curves under my hands, her full pouty lips, and those eyes that tore through my chest and saw deep into my soul. Her pull was magnetic, and I had no idea how I was going to convince her to let me in. I don't know when it happened, but somewhere along the line, home went from being a place to being with Delilah. I ached for her in ways I didn't think were possible. I don't know at what point baseball was no longer the most important thing in my life. Delilah was.

I shoved my hat down over my forehead, meeting a few guys hovering around the pitcher's mound, one new guy suited up in a practice uniform in their midst.

What the hell was this?

I hadn't been informed of a mid-season transfer, I didn't even know Coach had eyes on anyone.

As I drew closer, my eyes honed in on the shapely calves, a small waist…and I was sure I'd seen that curvy ass before.

"Delilah?"

"Check out the new teammate, Greenwood," Rod called, punching me on the shoulder.

"What are you doing?" I ignored him and focused my attention on Delilah.

Her eyes shot up to me, her lips curved into a small grin. "Guys asked me to throw a few balls. You know I can't run in a skirt."

"Well, no shit." I shook my head, enjoying the playful lilt in her voice. "Let's see what you got, Grey."

All the guys laughed, a few jogging off into their positions, more standing at the sidelines to watch the show. And little did I know what a show it was going to be.

"Scoot over, Greenwood." Delilah bumped her hip against me.

"Sure you're not gonna need a few pointers? A few warm-up throws?" I teased, enjoying every minute.

Delilah turned, planting her hands on her hips. The way the fine white threads pulled across her generous tits made my stomach churn with desire. She was so gorgeous, and the fact that the warm-up jersey fit her just right, the fabric tucked into her waist and pulling across every sexy curve she had, made me insane.

I wanted my hands on her now.

I needed to feel her again.

"Somethin' on your mind, Greenwood?"

"Just thinking how much better you'd look wrapped in my jersey."

Her eyes flared before she pushed me off the pitching mound. "In your dreams, playboy."

"Every night." I winked, enjoying her huffy attitude, wondering what she'd do if I said *to hell with everything* and pulled her in for a kiss right now.

But I couldn't do that, because I didn't trust myself to let her go.

"Watch and learn." Delilah smiled sweetly before turning, loosening her muscles as she made eye contact with Rod at home plate.

"Here we go," I said, just as she wound her arm back, wrist twisting just the slightest. The ball released, spinning as if in slow motion before slowing as it reached Rod. He swung low and missed it all together. "Holy shit."

"That's what I thought." Delilah smiled, and my dick pounded angrily in my pants. She was fucking good. How did she know how to throw a ball like that?

Delilah had severely understated her baseball experience, not only was she comfortable off the field, but the girl could kill it on the field, too.

Rod threw the ball back to her, and she caught it effortlessly in her glove.

I frowned. "Where'd you learn how to throw a ball like that?"

"Why? Want a few lessons?" Delilah cooed, then did a quick wind up and threw a fastball at Rod. This time he landed it squarely and drove the ball to left field.

"And here I was expecting you to throw like a girl." I knew that would rile her up.

"You're a chauvinistic bastard."

"And you're beautiful when you're angry." I stepped closer, my body drawn to hers like a magnet.

"You're..." She shoved her hands onto her hips again in her cute little defensive stance. "You're infuriating, Cash Greenwood."

Delilah walked off the mound, not even flinching when a ball whirred past her head, which was still covered in that cute little Timberwolves ball cap.

"You don't take well to compliments, do you?"

She didn't answer, just kept walking off the field and deep into the dark hall leading to the locker room.

"Your ass looks great in those pants." I followed her down the hallway.

Still she walked, her speed picking up.

"But the jersey would look better with my last name on it."

She entered the locker room and slammed the door behind her. Christ, I loved her spirit.

I entered behind her. "And I want those legs wrapped around me."

Delilah turned, tearing the ball cap off her head, long dark curls falling around her shoulders. "Listen here——"

I didn't give her a chance to speak. I crossed the distance between us, and my hands threaded through her hair, lips pressed against hers as we slammed into a row of old metal lockers. Delilah's hand curled around my neck, her leg hitched at my waist as I pushed my tongue past her lips. Her fucking taste drove white-hot need through to my balls, every nerve aching and strung tight waiting for release.

"I can't keep my hands off you."

She didn't answer, only pressed her lips to mine in a bruising kiss, her fingers pulling at the fine threads of my hair peeking out under my ball cap. My hands on her thighs, my thumbs digging into the flesh beneath the rough fabric of the warm-up pants. I'd been waiting for this, for her, I just hadn't known it.

I'd seen my parents ruined by addiction, so I'd steered far clear of anything that could mess with my head, including love. But this wasn't love yet was it? How could it be?

But how could it not be?

I shook my head, inhaling a breath of her intoxicating scent.

"I can smell how much you want me," I growled, and a small moan fell past her lips. Her head thrown back against the locker, she clutched at my biceps hard enough I was sure there would be bruises tomorrow. I didn't give a fuck. I wanted her marks all over me. Since she already consumed my thoughts, why not wear her badge on my body?

My mind roared at me to claim her, shove inside her and fuck until we were both exhausted and desperate for more. I was sure of one thing: having Delilah Grey once wouldn't be enough. The idea of losing myself in her every day sent unfamiliar waves of contentment rolling through my body.

"I want to sink inside you right here, right now," I whispered, trailing my nose down the long line of her neck. Her hips arched, my cock making contact with the hot seam of her pussy through our clothing and making my mind hazy with crazed lust. I nipped at the soft flesh of her neck. "I want to leave my mark on you."

"I don't know why I keep subjecting myself to you," she finally responded, her lips covering mine in quick kisses.

"Because you can't help yourself?" My hands danced across her body, skimming the swell of her beautiful tits. "I want you addicted to my touch."

"I don't get addicted to anything, or anyone."

"Not until now, you haven't." I kneaded the flesh of her breast beneath the shirt as I ran my cotton-covered cock between her thighs. "I can't stop thinking about you. You're like a drug, Delilah."

"Hey! Greenwood, where'd ya disappear to, man?!" Rod burst through the doors, and like I'd burned her, Delilah dropped from my body, turning back to the locker she'd been digging in.

I shook my head, eyes darting from her to Rod. "Comin', bro."

Rod's eyes narrowed at Delilah's ass propped in the air as she was bent, digging through her bag.

"Hey, eyes up, fucker."

Rod's face split into a grin. "Gotcha, man."

He backed out of the doors, making an obscene gesture with his hands the entire way. I flipped him off before the door swung closed.

"You should go." Delilah turned, her clothes clutched to her chest and hiding her beautiful self from me.

"I don't want to." I advanced on her, catching her chin in my fingers.

"But you should." She pulled away from my grip, eyes averting to the floor. "I'm gonna get changed, so…"

I huffed, my cock desperate to find itself between her thighs again. Images of her naked swirled in my head, and I knew I'd have to leave ASAP if I had any hope of reining myself in.

"I'll catch you after practice? Maybe we could grab something to eat."

"Maybe." She bit down on her bottom lip, and I knew then it wouldn't happen. There was still something holding her back, despite her body screaming *yes*, despite the way she shivered and moaned when I touched her.

"I'll be waiting, Delilah. Whenever you're ready, I'll be waiting." I trailed my thumb across the bow of her top lip, watching as her eyes fell closed and her cheeks burned crimson. Before she could respond, I turned, heading for the swinging doors. "Later, Grey."

8

Delilah

"Most of the guys are gone by now," I uttered to Tori, one of my closest friends. I'd managed to grab her an extra ticket to tonight's game, which the Timberwolves had won. "You'll get to meet a few of them, though."

"What about that one who keeps shoving his tongue down your throat?" Tori's eyes sparkled back at me just as the door swung open and Rod walked out of the locker room. His hair was still damp from his shower, his skin a warm cocoa, with the darkest eyelashes I'd ever seen on a man. He was gorgeous, his jawline strong, cheekbones high. I could see why preteen girls taped posters of him on their walls, but he was so cocky, so shameless. He wasn't anyone I could ever date. Alarm bells rang loud and clear when he was in the room.

"Hey, Grey."

"Hey—"

"I'm Tori Fountain." My sweet, overly friendly friend burst between us, hand thrust out. "I'm Delilah's bestie. Can we get a selfie?"

I rolled my eyes, but Rodriguez swung an arm around Tori, tucking her in close under his arm as she fumbled for her phone. "I can take the picture if you want."

"No, I want a selfie." Tori puckered her lips. Her blush deepened, her eyes glazing just a little when Rodriguez sent her a panty-melting half-grin.

I nearly threw up in my mouth.

Tori grinned wildly as they posed for the photo.

"They're a pair." Cash's voice warmed my insides.

I sucked in a breath, trying to rid my mind of all the intoxicating thoughts that buzzed when he was around. "I shouldn't have brought her back here."

"Probably not your smartest move," Cash said.

I shot him a glare, crossing my arms.

"Great game tonight, guys," Tori crooned, eyes dancing from Cash to Rodriguez.

"Sure it woulda been better if we would have had this arm." Cash's hand curled around my bicep and sent a current of arousal straight between my thighs. "Didn't know you had it in you, champ."

"Of course she does. She's like baseball royalty." Tori grinned, and I sighed, thinking I didn't want to get into that conversation now, or ever.

"Royalty?" I caught Cash's arched eyebrow.

"Her dad, her granddad, even her godfather. It's, like, a dynasty," Tori sputtered on to my horror. She always got too chatty when she was nervous, but why did it have to be about me this particular time?

"She's been drinking, don't listen to her." I grumbled, digging in my purse for my phone so I could pretend I had an urgent reason to get the hell out of there.

"You guys wanna do dinner tonight? I could eat a fucking pig," Rodriguez belted.

"That sounds great!" Tori replied, and I tensed.

"Are you sure? Didn't you say you had something to do tonight?" I shot Tori a serious glance.

"No, not till later. Plus, I'm starving." She grinned, glancing over at Rodriguez.

"I can get us reservations," Cash interjected, pulling out his phone.

"No, you guys go on—"

"Call that Brazilian place, Greenwood."

"I've got reservations for four at a Japanese steakhouse." Cash swiped his thumb, then smiled and pocketed his phone. "They've got a floating floor—fish swim right under your table."

"Sounds great. Whaddya say, ladies?" Rodriguez held out his hand, flashing Tori another one of his trademark grins, making her swoon. I nearly died of embarrassment. I didn't want to go to this dinner for two reasons, one, the hormonal display of crazy happening in front of me sounded like the worst way to spend my night, and two, Cash's palm at my back, pushing me ahead of him down the hallway proved I couldn't control myself with him. It was taking everything in me to not stop in my tracks, turn around, and beg him to kiss me.

My heart thudded hopelessly in my chest as Cash and I followed Tori and Rodriguez through the parking garage.

I didn't know what I'd gotten myself into, but it was proving to be the start of an interesting night for sure.

Twenty minutes later, after a heart-dropping and dangerous ride through the city, we arrived to a trendy new restaurant on the other side of town. A valet opened the door of Rodriguez's Spider and we all filed out.

Cash's palm hovering at my waist protectively sent butterflies scurrying in my stomach. I couldn't deny that I loved his touch on me, but every smart brain cell in my head was telling me that he was all wrong. It took a special kind of woman to love a star athlete, one who could handle millions of other woman ogling their man, and that woman wasn't me.

"This is great, isn't it?" Cash pulled me closer to him as we stepped through the doors. A dim, blue-lit space opened up around us. And the floor. The floor was one long pool of crystal blue, all kinds of fish in a rainbow of colors swimming beneath the clear glass.

"This is incredible." I stepped in, feeling instantly underdressed, even though I was already in business attire for work.

"Great call, man." Rodriguez patted Cash on the shoulder as we were seated at an intimate table for four in a far corner. I glanced around, noticing most of the tables around us were occupied by couples on dates. We were all out of place here. The guys were still fresh from showers, and while they looked handsome in dark jeans and slim-cut button-downs, most of the men here were wearing suits and ties.

I mustered a smile when Cash pulled out my chair. He was going to get all the wrong ideas from this, and I was going to fall a little deeper under his spell. I should have bailed and grabbed a taxi home, eaten takeout, and caught the replays on ESPN. I had no business having an intimate dinner with Cash fucking Greenwood, star Major League pitcher.

"Relax, Grey." Cash draped an arm across my shoulder, sliding his thumb around the base of my neck. My eyes shuttered closed, my heart hammering uncontrollably as I thought of us here, together. His hands on me. I sucked in a fortifying breath, which sent a blast of his spicy soap straight to my head.

"Something to drink?" the waiter asked. I nodded, my brain foggy at the proximity of Cash. Why couldn't I control myself around him? Why was he doing this to me?

"You doin' okay?" Cash's breath washed across my neck, the hair feathering across my skin with his words.

"I'm okay," I finally responded. I hoped he could hear over the hammering of my heart.

"You look beautiful." Cash trailed a fingertip across my collarbone, visible just above the frilly neckline of my blouse.

I struggled to control my voice. "Thank you."

"We should have them take a picture of us!" Tori called, jumping up and flagging down a waiter. I smiled genuinely when Cash tucked me in closer to his body as we posed. The flash nearly blinded me, but I prayed the picture was a good one. I knew I'd cherish it, because despite everything between Cash and me, he'd had an impact on me, this entire team had. While Rodriguez could be cocky and mouthy sometimes, that was the biggest problem they had. Nothing beyond healthy competition and positivity radiated from this team, and they deserved to go all the way to the World Series.

"So, what got you into baseball?" Tori asked sweetly.

"It's the only thing we had in Cuba. Every night I was out at the corner ball field, playing with the old guys. My dad didn't have much time, he worked too much, but there were always guys at the field. My momma always knew where to find me." Rodriguez tapped his forehead, emotion warm in his dark eyes.

"Kinda the same for me, too," Cash chimed in. "My dad wasn't around a lot. In fact, baseball was about all we had to talk about. I remember getting three home runs on my little league team one day. He was so proud of me. I was only eight, but I swear, that look drove me forward."

My hand instinctively went to his thigh under the table. I wasn't thinking, only knew that he was revealing something special about himself, and acknowledging it felt like the only thing I could do.

Cash turned to me, eyes burning up mine. "What about you? What brought you to the ball field?"

"I feel like I've never had a choice." I answered, unfiltered, then regretted it. "I mean, family or work, I keep finding myself in a baseball diamond, no matter what I do." I tried to laugh off the comment, but it fell on silent ears. I'd said more about myself than I'd ever intended to. Tori knew my entire history, but it'd taken her years for me to open up and tell her all the details.

"You were born to be on a ball field." Cash fingered a wisp of my hair, sending the edges tickling along my skin. A cool chill raced through me, and I shifted, distracted by the arousal dampening my thighs.

"I don't know about *born to be on a ball field*, but there is something about it that feels like home. I swear I didn't think I'd ever take a job with a baseball team. I'd done every single other sport, but I couldn't pass this one up for some reason…" I trailed off, smiling up at the waiter as he set glasses of water on the table.

"I wanna hear more about this baseball royalty thing. I want names, Grey," Rodriguez shot across the table.

"No way," I laughed.

"Delilah doesn't tell anyone. I didn't even know who her dad was for years! That bitch left me hanging!" Tori giggled.

"It's true." I looked at Cash. "I don't tell a soul."

"I'll get it out of you."

"You think so?" I crooked a grin at him.

"I know so," he promised, sending molten lava through my veins.

"What makes you so confident?" I shot back.

"I've got a lot of talents, Ms. Grey." A shudder raced through my system at his words.

For some reason I believed him.

Cash slipped a thumb under the neckline of my shirt, causing my breath to stick in my throat.

I had a feeling I was going to discover just what those talents were.

9

Cash

"Mornin', beautiful."

"Oh my god, this again?" Delilah rolled her pretty eyes. Dinner had gone amazing last night, and while she'd opened up a little, I could still tell she was holding back on me. This girl was making me work for it, that was for sure, but there was something down deep that pulled at my insides whenever she was around.

"What ya up to?" I landed in the bleacher seat next to her.

"What's your best guess, Greenwood?"

The way her mouth curled up at the corner made my dick ache. "I was gonna guess you came to check out ball

79

players."

"Because it's my job." She shot me a sideways glance. "And you're being distracting."

"Wouldn't know what else to do with my time." I shrugged, crossing my arms and ankles before propping my legs up on the seat in front of me.

"There's got to be a million other things you can do besides bother me."

"You wound my heart!" I clutched at my chest.

"I bet." Her eyes narrowed, but her smile deepened. I loved that look on her face because I was the one who had put it there, and I damn sure planned to put a few more there.

"I've got nothing better to do with my time than watch a few players practice with the prettiest girl I've ever seen."

Delilah's eyes widened before her gaze turned back to the field. She held a pencil in her hand, tapping the eraser against her knee as she fidgeted.

"Everything about you draws me in, Delilah." I stroked my fingertips up the line of her thigh, watching a visible shudder roll through her system as she shifted in her seat. "What happened last night, I want it to happen again." I reached her waist, trailing a fingertip across the waistband of her pants before darting beneath the fabric.

She licked her perky lips, her mouth parting just slightly with soft breaths. I glanced around the field, thankful as fuck she'd chosen this dark little corner to watch warm-ups from. We were so far out of anyone's line of sight, we virtually had the stadium to ourselves.

"I want to taste this pretty pussy," I whispered as I drew a deft fingertip over the crotch of her panties. Her back arched in the stadium seat, the fabric of her shirt pulling across her tits and making me so fucking horny I thought I might die

Unable to hold back a minute more, I lunged across the seat, caging her in my arms and ducking to taste her lips. I worked the delicate little bud of her clit through her panties while my tongue darted into her mouth, swirling and tasting the decadent flavors. One of her arms wrapped around my neck as her leg hitched around my hip, her body ebbing and flowing against me like a wild wave.

"Christ, you're responsive." My palm trailed up her torso, pushing under her shirt and gripping at the flesh of one full tit. Soft whimpers escaped her throat when I slipped a thumb inside the lacy little bra and fingered her taut nipple. "You're the sexiest thing I've ever seen."

"I can't believe we're doing this," she whispered through agonized pants.

"We can't keep our hands off each other. We were stupid to think it wouldn't happen," I nipped at the plump flesh of her bottom lip.

"I'm going to tell myself whatever I have to in the morning to forget this even happened." Her eyes flared before she pulled my head down to hers, pressing ours lips together in a bruising kiss.

"Tell yourself whatever you have to, but right now you're mine. I know for a fact that the security cameras are only on during games. We're safe here, baby."

"Oh my god," she breathed when I yanked the pants and panties from her waist, giving me enough room to angle between her thighs.

"This is fucking beautiful." I pushed her thighs apart, my gaze falling on her glistening pink pussy as every corded muscle in my body bunched and pulled, my cock flexing and wanting nothing more than to sink in and fuck her until neither of us could see straight.

My eyes connected with hers in that moment, and before she could even open her pretty lips, I grinned and dove in, trailing my tongue up and down her slit, then swirling at her pussy. Delilah's hands clutched at my hair, my scalp burning with the pull of her grasp, and my dick pounding with every fucking heartbeat.

"Sweeter than honey, baby." I sucked the bud of her clit into my mouth and drew in long pulls, enjoying every ounce of her body gyrating underneath mine.

Delilah's free hand trailed her body, turning me on with every stroke, when I laced our fingers together. Both of our palms molded the flesh of her breast, forcing our fingertips to pinch at the dark little nipples before I flicked my tongue, then danced one long finger at her entrance.

"I can't wait to bury myself inside this body, but not here. I want you all to myself the first time. An entire night. Maybe even the whole weekend." I kneaded her gorgeous tit again before sliding my finger into her hot, wet body, feeling her spasm around my fingers, I hooked and worked my tongue at her clit before her thighs clenched around my shoulders, passion-fueled moans burning past her lips with her orgasm.

"You are my favorite thing first thing in the morning." I grinned, making a point of wiping her pussy off my face, then sliding my thumb between my lips and licking it off.

"Cash, oh my god." She attempted to cover her face before I caught her hands, pushing them around my neck before kissing the frown off her face.

"Don't hide yourself from me, not ever. Got that,

Delilah?"

"You're crazy, Cash Greenwood."

"Only for you." I winked at her as I pulled her pants up her legs, rearranging her panties and putting her back together.

"I can't believe you did that."

"We. We did that." I sat back in my seat, catching her hand in mine as I did. "And get used to it, Delilah. I've been fucking starved for you, and this barely even scratched the surface."

10

Delilah

My heart drummed frantic beats in my ears as his words echoed on repeat. What was he thinking? What was I thinking?

As if my surroundings were suddenly coming into focus for the first time, I glanced around at the players tossing balls on the field, a few others swinging bats as they warmed up their muscles.

"Cash..." I shook my head, suddenly feeling a wave of fear wash through me. I knew where this led, no point in taking it any further. A groupie tomorrow, another one the next day, my heart left bleeding out in the dirt. No way was that life for me.

"Oh, no you don't. I know that look on your face." Cash stood, placing a delicate kiss on my knuckles before backing away. "I'm leaving before you say something I'm gonna regret hearing. We both know that whatever you say today isn't going to make a damn bit of difference tomorrow when we see each other." He hummed against my ear and sent shockwaves through my body. "Have a great day, Ms. Grey."

I swallowed, pushing a hand through my hair. My mind reeled as he walked away. He'd stopped me before I could even get a word out. He knew me so well already, knew that my irrational fears would get the better of me and my defense mechanisms would do their best to send him packing. But that hadn't happened. He'd cut me off, and somewhere deep down inside, I liked it. He'd stopped my stupid emotional trigger in its tracks and left me thinking maybe what we had was different from anything I'd ever known. I only had to give it a chance.

I sighed, throwing my bag over my shoulder. I needed a hot shower to shake Cash's talented tongue and those incredibly long fingers from my mind. I sped down the long hallway, turning the corner just as I ran into a wall of a body.

A body that reeked of whiskey.

"Hey, why the rush?" Rodriguez's hands came around my shoulders. He was clearly unsteady on his feet.

"What are you thinking? I'm disappointed in you, Rodriguez. You're not gonna get your stats up if you're more concerned with partying. Go home and get some rest." I pulled away from him, taking a step back and right into Cash's broad chest.

"What's up, Rod?"

"Just seein' where your girl is off to. I don't think she likes me very much." Rodriguez glanced from Cash to me.

"I think she's right. You need to go sleep this one off. I'll stop by later for pizza and we can talk about the game." Cash clapped his teammate on the shoulder.

"Nah, man. Don't need your help." Rodriguez shrugged Cash off.

"Like hell you don't. If you don't sober up, Coach is going to bench you the rest of the season and force you into rehab, man. You know that."

"Fuck off."

"He's right. You're off your game; the numbers show it," I offered, not wanting to push too much but knowing Rodriguez had too much talent to drink it away. Just like someone else I knew.

"Here, let me get you home." Cash clasped a hand around Rodriguez's shoulder, shot me one last long look, and led him down the long hallway.

The depth of Cash's compassion astounded me. I'd never met anyone like him, much less a ball player. They were usually so self-involved they couldn't see beyond their own ego, but Cash put everyone first. Even me.

I sighed, watching them leave, glad that Rodriguez had a friend like Cash to help him when he was down. We could all use someone like that in our lives.

Later that night, long after the game and the little run-in with Rodriguez, I turned the corner in the hotel, thinking I should do some packing if I had any chance of making the early flight in the morning, and I heard a voice murmuring low.

I frowned, stalling when I turned the corner to find Cash leaning against the wall near my room, speaking into his phone. I hadn't seen him since our tryst in the bleachers this morning, but now he looked upset. Really upset. His brow was furrowed, and a deep frown marred his normally relaxed face.

I almost turned to leave, trying to avoid betraying his privacy, then thought better, frowning as I moved closer, my hotel key already out and ready to swipe.

Cash's eyes rolled up my body as soon as I was close, his darkened irises landing on mine and swimming with something painful. His look swept the breath from my lungs, and I knew instantly I couldn't leave him, because whatever that phone call was about, it wasn't good.

Cash murmured something else before promising to do what he could, then hanging up the phone.

"Are you okay?"

Cash froze, no words falling from his lips before I dropped my bag on the floor, not even sure what I was doing beyond comforting him the only way I knew how. I wrapped my arms around his shoulders, and his arms encircled me, and we held each other. He held me so tightly for long minutes, I thought he might crush the air from my lungs, but it was the best hug I'd ever received.

Warmth rolled in waves from him to me, and before I knew what was happening, Cash's hands were crawling up my skin, his lips tracing mine, and his tongue pressed at the seam of my mouth. I opened, and our tongues tangled intimately, my brain blurring with images of earlier images of him, images of us, together.

Without words he lifted me into his arms, taking my keycard in one hand and swiping it at the door before it buzzed and we crashed into my hotel room. He dropped me on my feet, and without thinking, with all the pent-up energy from the orgasm earlier and the memory of his hands and his lips on me, I pulled my top over my head and stood in the middle of the floor in my pants and a bra.

Cash's eyes narrowed, and he pulled his own shirt over his head, then pushed his hands through my hair, and we both fell down onto the fluffy bed. "I need us tonight."

"Yes, yes," I gasped against his lips, my hands tugging his hair, the scent of him surrounding me and sending my mind hazy with lust. Cash's lips kissed across my collarbone, then he drew his tongue over the flesh of my breasts, pushing the straps down my arms. With frantic movements, he shoved my pants and panties down my legs, grazing his fingertips across my bare pussy before nestling his hips between my thighs. The hot, thick ridge of his cock pressed against my clit and sent me arching up on the bed, desperate for more of him now.

I didn't know what we were doing, I didn't know what I was thinking, because this was certainly not the place I expected to be tonight, but I was sick and tired of denying whatever this was between us. In the far reaches of my mind, I thought maybe this would satisfy the itch. Maybe we could do this tonight, then wake up tomorrow satisfied, the banter and sexual tension no longer pulsing uncontrollably between us.

"You make me crazy, Delilah." He hooked a hand behind my head and brought his lips to mine, kissing me until I was breathless, bruising my lips until only the memory of him remained. Cash pulled the waistband of his workout pants down his thighs, and suddenly his cock was right there, pressed against me, sliding along the slit of my pussy, sending me into another world with frenzied need.

"I don't want a single thing separating me from you." Cash's words made my stomach flutter. I'd never felt so wanted on such a primal level. His hands clutched at my hips as he lined his cock up with my entrance, his eyes searing into me, dark with lust and barely contained need. "You drive me fucking insane, but I can't stop thinking about you." In the next breath he was pushing into me, my body stretching around him as he caressed every inch of skin he could reach.

"I..." I sighed, struggling for words. "I've never been with anyone Cash... Only you." Shallow breaths punctuated my words as every slow centimeter of him filled me. I arched, digging my nails into his back as his lips melded with mine. I was his, the touch of his lips and the press of his fingers on my body confirmed it. The pinch and burn of his cock stretching my insides, his body breaching mine for the first time, everything about him left me breathless and craving more.

He kissed me in measured strokes as his dick delved deeper inside my body. "We're each other's first, and each other's last."

Cash was made for me, our bodies meeting and reacting like chemicals, the reaction too explosive to ignore, burning up the space between us and creating something new and irrevocably bonded.

There would be no going back for us.

Cash's hips sped up, his rhythm matching mine as we tangled on the sheets, sweat and sex scenting the air while his hands crawled over my body, owning every inch of me as if he was leaving a brand on my skin. "Christ, you don't know what it does to me to know I've the only man that's been here."

My heart thrummed in my chest at his words. I knew them to be true, this night would make us more desperate for each other.

"I want you now," I moaned as his hands clutched my hips and he drove me to the edge.

"I want every day with you, Delilah. We're nowhere near done yet." He pulled me from the bed, lifting me in his arms and pushing me up against the cool glass of the French doors that led to a balcony.

Hitching my legs over his hips, he slid his cock deep into my body, every cell screaming for more, harder, faster, now. "I'm going to fuck you until you can't think straight, Delilah. I'm going to fuck you until you can't form a word with that pretty, sassy mouth of yours."

I pushed my hands through his hair, then attached my lips to his, loving every combustible moment of his skin against mine.

"I can take care of you, Delilah." He accented my name with a ragged thrust. "I can give you everything."

Tears burned behind my eyelids as I clutched at the threads of his hair, one of his hands sliding down between us and swirling at my clit. "I want your cum all over my dick."

I gnashed my teeth as his thumb sped up and the sensations overtook my body.

"Cum, gorgeous."

My muscles tensed as release crashed through me. My toes curled and my breaths heaved as waves of pleasure seared every nerve.

"You and me, Delilah, we're forever." Cash's lips caught mine as he plunged his tongue between them and fucked me as his body shuddered and slowed, his release emptying into me in powerful waves. He wrapped his arms around my body, his head falling on my shoulder as he sucked in the flesh at the curve of my neck. "You taste like heaven."

I was unable to form words, my body overwhelmed by his touch, my mind raging with his all-consuming attention. Everything he did and said was right. He was perfect.

But no one was perfect.

Something had to mess this up. I didn't believe in fairy tales, and Cash Greenwood was not my Prince Charming, no matter how much he tried to be.

"You're thinking again, Grey," Cash murmured against the shell of my ear, sending a shiver through me.

"It's a curse." I smiled ruefully, then placed a quick kiss on his chin.

"You're my curse." The slow drag of Cash's cock as he pulled out of me sent leftover sensations pulsing through me. "But it just so happens I love being wrapped up in you."

"You're a charmer, Cash Greenwood." I rolled my eyes.

"Only for you, Delilah. Only for you."

11

Cash

I woke up later that night, untangling myself from the beautiful girl I'd fallen into bed with in an act of quiet desperation last night. Delilah's silky hair spread out on the pillow around her, the sheet slipping off her body to reveal her sweet curves, she was a slice of Heaven.

Just looking at her now made my stomach twist with desire to protect her, and make her happy. I remembered reading somewhere that we were all in search of someone whose demons play well with ours, but in my case Delilah cast out my demons. Everything that haunted me and had me running from my life, she dulled. With her by my side, none of it mattered anymore. The only thing that mattered was her. My whole life I was searching for the light, and in Delilah I finally found blinding peace.

I loved the way she twisted her lips in a cocky grin when something was on her mind, I loved teasing her and listening to her laugh. I loved her hands touching me; it felt like silk caressing my skin. I loved making love to her. I loved seeing the way we fit perfectly when we made love, until I lost the concept of where she began and I ended. It wasn't me and her anymore, it was *us*.

I loved everything about her.

Which is what made this next part so complicated.

I snagged my phone off the table, then headed for the balcony, stepping outside in the cool air to clear my head. I had to do something about the phone call I'd received earlier. Falling into bed with Delilah wasn't exactly dealing with it. I typed a few terms into the search bar, looking for ideas on how best to help the situation. It wasn't a new one, I'd been getting calls just like this for years, I was just sick of never finding a resolution to all the pain that seemed to follow me.

"Everything okay?" Delilah's angelic voice whispered. There she was, stepping onto the balcony to join me.

"Mmm, I'm perfect." I sat down and pulled her into my lap. With the sheet wrapped around her body, I wanted to unwrap her, kiss every inch of her skin and make love to her all over again. "You smell like me." I loved that. I loved that her scent was now mixed with mine, like I had marked her. In some weird way, I was proud. I was proud that this amazing woman with so much passion, strength, and beauty would let me in. She welcomed me into her warmth and I was determined to show her, for the rest of my life, just how much I worshiped her. She would never again be lonely, scared, or want for anything. I would let her know just how much she meant to me. Every breath I took would be for her, every action, every thought for her and her alone.

Delilah's smile deepened as her eyes closed and she nestled into my neck. Stray strands of her hair danced on the breeze and curled around my face. Christ, how I loved having her in my arms.

"What are you doing out here?" Delilah asked.

I sighed, hesitant to unload all of my baggage on her at once. "Got a phone call from home. My dad needs some help."

"Is he okay?" The concern bleeding from her eyes cracked open my heart.

"He's okay right now, but I guess he's having some issues…" I paused, unsure of how to say the next part.

"You can tell me, no judgement." She smiled softly before pressing a kiss to my lips.

"My dad is an alcoholic." I thrust a hand through my hair. "I've been sending him money, more than enough to cover his bills, but apparently he's not paying them. He's behind on the mortgage. I knew I should have just paid it off, but he insisted he didn't want my money. God knows what he's been doing with the money every month, but one of his buddies gave me a call and said he's been hanging out at the local casino," I finished, feeling a little lighter for having shared it with someone.

"I'm so sorry." Delilah pushed a piece of hair off my forehead. I was so glad she was here. Going back to my room alone last night had felt like a nightmare. I wanted to lose myself in her, forget about all the tough stuff and just be us together.

"I don't know what to do. The old man is so stubborn. It's like he almost resents it when I offer to help."

"Has he ever gone to an AA meeting? Maybe that could help…"

"Nah, he refuses. People like him don't need community support, he likes to say. I don't get it, but what I know for sure is this isn't the right path. I haven't even been to see him in over a year, says he's too busy for company."

"Cash…that's terrible."

"I'm used to it. He's been this way most my life. That's even the reason I started playing baseball. It was his favorite sport. The only time we ever spent time together was in front of the TV watching the game. I thought if I played, he'd hang out with me more, be proud of me, and for a while he was, at least I think so, but the older he got, the more he started drinking, the less he cared. Then baseball became my escape, suddenly it was something that was mine, and I didn't want him to have anything to do with it. Thank God for practice six nights a week—it kept me out of that house where he was drinking himself to death."

"What does your mom think?"

I looked up at the spray of silver stars in the sky and closed my eyes. "She died when I was fifteen. A massive heart attack. He's been worse since."

Without words, Delilah wrapped her arms around my neck, holding on tightly as my hands trailed around her back. I sucked in a deep breath, memories of little league and home runs and hotdogs flooding my memories. Dad hadn't always been there, sometimes too drunk to even wake up in time, but Mom had always gone. She'd sit in the bleachers every game those first few years, cheering me on, until life had gotten the best of her. My mother was such a gentle and beautiful woman. I missed her. I missed the sound of her voice, the way she always smelled like fresh-cut violets, I even missed how she would scold me. I just missed her.

I'd raised myself after she died. My father had never really been a dad, but my mom, she always made sure that I did the right thing, pushing me to succeed in life. When she died I could have gone in so many directions, but to honor her memory, I did the right things. I never wanted my mother to be ashamed of me. I hoped that, wherever she was, she was smiling down on me and proud of the man she raised me to become.

"How can we help your dad?" Delilah asked a few minutes later.

"Well, I'm gonna call the bank in the morning and get his payments straightened out. I'll probably just pay off the damn house. I'm so sick of dealing with this. And then I don't have to worry about sending him checks that he's spending God knows where. But he won't go to rehab, Delilah, I know him..."

"Maybe he could talk to an addiction specialist. Send one to his house, even just to get a read on his situation."

I nodded, her words sinking in. "That's a good idea, I don't even think he'd let me in the house if I went."

"You send him a check every month, but he won't talk to you?"

I shook my head, feeling the sting of what seemed an impossible situation. "Sometimes it's easier to say nothing, I guess."

"I know what you mean." Her eyes turned away, her fingers twisting together before she continued. "My dad played ball for a lot of years. My entire life was spent on the ball field, and it seemed like he didn't want anything to do with us unless we were talking about baseball. He let the life get the best of him." Delilah peered up at me. "My dad spent the offseason drunk, running around on my mom. I think he figured life wasn't worth it if he wasn't playing baseball." Her beautiful lips turned down sadly, and I wanted to kiss that sadness right off her face. "There were always guys over at the house all hours of the night, I even caught him stumbling and drunk with a groupie one night. It was bad. I swore I'd never subject myself to that once I was old enough to leave. I swore I wouldn't find myself in my mom's position, trying to tame a wild animal. He shouldn't have had a family. He didn't know how to love them enough."

I traced circles on her wrist, wishing more than anything I could find a way to take away her pain. It all made so much sense now, the chip on her shoulder, her aversion to ball players. She wasn't kidding when she said she had triggers, it was clear the scars from her past were deep. "You didn't deserve that, Delilah."

She pushed a stray lock of hair behind her ear, looking everywhere but at me.

"Hey," I caught her chin between my fingers. "I mean it, and I can promise you I'm not that guy."

"They all say that." Her grin twisted ruefully.

"But they don't all mean it."

Delilah nodded, her eyes following mine before I wrapped her in my arms again, pulling her against my body and kissing her. "Let's forget about that right now. I've got you here, and I want to take advantage."

Delilah giggled when I lifted her in my arms, standing from the chair and carrying her back into the bedroom. "I have to say, I kind of like you taking advantage of me."

"Good, I need to do it a lot more." I swallowed her giggle with my kiss, and just like that, I was lost in her again.

We all have an addiction, and Delilah was mine.

12

Delilah

As the summer heat faded to a cool fall, the Timberwolves burned up the scoreboard, landing themselves at the top of their league. They'd won game after game for weeks, and if they maintained this pace, if I could continue to analyze the figures and get the right players in the right position at the right time, we could win the pennant, then go on to the World Series.

Navy blanketed the sky when I finally packed up my laptop, picking my way down the stands to head back home after another game. The stadium was empty, the quiet oddly comforting long after the lights were switched off. I hit the turf and turned the corner into the hallway that lead to the underbelly of the stadium when I ran a rock-hard body.

"Coach said you hadn't left yet." Cash's hands held my face and kissed me long and slow, butterflies battering up my throat as I wrapped my arms around his neck and pulled him closer to me.

"Come with me," he breathed, snagging my hand with his.

"Bossy, huh, Greenwood?" I teased, but followed him anyway.

"I am, when I know what I want."

"And that is?" I baited him.

Cash stopped when we reached the turf behind the pitcher's mound. Caressing my face, he was kissing me again, fingertips working into my hair as our mouths connected. I slid my hands between us, working the button of his baseball pants open, then peeling the metal teeth of the zipper apart one by one.

"What are you doing, Delilah?" His ravaged voice caressed my ears.

"I want to drive you crazy." I dropped to my knees, slipping my hand in his pants and pulling his cock free. Thick and rock hard, I wrapped my fist around the base, watching it jerk with the cool air and my touch. Adrenaline fueled my desire at the thought of getting caught.

"You already drive me crazy," Cash's hips worked back and forth impulsively.

"Then hold on, Greenwood." I grinned up at him before trailing my tongue up the beautiful curve of his thick cock. Swirling along the ridge at his tip, he sucked in a violent breath before his hands twined into my hair, holding me still.

Fisting my hand around his girth, I sucked my cheeks and pressed the tip of his cock to the back of my throat, swallowing and enjoying the smooth groove of his searing hot erection. I then pressed a hand between his legs, cupping his heavy sac in my hand. Cash's legs shook, his hands gripping at my temples as the sharp angle of his jaw hardened with barely held control.

"I can't take your lips on me, sweetheart. It's too much." Heat radiated from his touch, making me feel warm and safe and so loved. "I want to see you." He slipped out of my mouth and pushed me into the grass, his fingers already thumbing the buttons through their holes on my shirt, pushing the fabric off my shoulders.

I suddenly felt so vulnerable. "What if there's someone here still?"

"They can't even see us out here, baby. All the lights are off. They'd have to stumble over us to even notice." His hands pulling down my pants in the next breath.

Cool air caressed my skin sending shudders through my body as his knuckles brushed against me. Cash's fingers slid down my pants and swirled arousal at the burning bud of my clit. I arched, pushing my fingers through the strands of his hair when his lips attached at my throat and sucked. Desire surged through me, tingling and burning up my skin and making me feel a thousand different feelings in one moment.

"I'm useless when your hands are on me."

One of his fingers plunged into my body, the invasion erotic as nerves burned up with exquisite fire.

"That means I'm doing my job, then." His fingers

pushed in and out of my pussy, his thumb swirling in fierce circles at my clit. Soft moans charged past my lips as all the sensations flooding through me became too intense. My legs shook and my fingernails crushed his shirt as I rode the rhythm of his hand, chasing a wave of pleasure and coming ever closer to the crest.

Cash moved down my body, his nose tracing the indentation of my navel before hovering over the bare skin of my pussy. He inhaled sharply, eyes burning as the peered back at me before sliding his tongue between my thighs. With his fingers pressing into my body, his tongue running flat against my clit, my nerves hummed with fire until he drew a swift orgasm out of me. My chest heaving, I came down from a high like I'd never experienced before, his hands roaming up my skin and kissing my lips before I could even recover.

"I used to think baseball was the only thing I loved." Cash caught my lips with his, my arousal climbing higher with the taste of me on him. "But now it's you. I don't want anything between us." His cock pushed past my entrance, my body pulsing with every nerve he touched.

"I haven't been with anyone, just you, Cash." I moaned when he seated himself inside me, his hands clutching at my hips and holding me in place, his knees digging into the turf as he pumped, his cock driving me to the jagged edge. Cash hooked my knees around his biceps and pushed me further into the grass, every inch of my skin buzzing with lust as his lips trailed down my neck, his mouth sucking at my collarbone. One hand slipped between us and he was thumbing my clit again.

"Come on my cock, Delilah. Soak me."

My teeth clamped down as his thumb sped up, his cock angled and hitting a bundle of nerves I didn't even know existed. My nails dug into the flesh of his back, his thumbs gripping my hips so firmly I thought he might leave bruises. His marks.

Delicious coils of lust unfurled in my belly at the thought. I wanted to be his, I loved the thought of wearing a piece of him on me. My heart battered my rib cage wildly as his tongue traced down my neck, between the flesh of my breasts, swirling at my cleavage and catching a nipple between his teeth.

His dark eyes shimmered up at me, his hips sped up and he angled the base of his cock at just the right angle to grate perfectly across my clit.

I sucked in frantic gulps of air, his body hard and damp with sex as he sucked on my nipple, jagged thrusts driving me over the edge. A tornado of lust spun through my head as his thighs held him firmly, his cock jerking with waves of release. I could show him what my words couldn't say. He could feel it in those moments pulsing between us.

"So fucking beautiful. Everything about you," he murmured, his lips working against my skin. "You make everything better."

I hummed, trailing my fingertips across his shoulder before he leaned against me, caging me in his arms and making me feel more loved and protected than I ever had. I didn't know these feelings could exist, I'd spent so much of my life protecting myself, building walls and keeping men out, that I hadn't stopped to think that maybe someone else could do a better job.

"Let's go back to my place." Cash threaded our fingers together and traced my knuckles with kisses.

"I should go home..." I trailed off, not ready to leave him yet. If ever.

"No fucking way, babe. My home is yours now."

"You're insane, Cash," I giggled, though warmth coated my stomach at his words.

"Really fucking insane...for you." He placed a kiss on my lips, pulling my pants back up my legs. "Get used to it."

It may have been dark in that field, but I swear I saw his eyes sparkle with those words. And I believed him. For the first time in so long, I gave myself up to fate, followed my heart, and believed him.

13

Delilah

"To play-offs!" Rod held a shot in the air, a small group to guys toasting around the hotel bar. They'd won the last regular season game tonight, solidifying their spot as lead champs, with only play-offs to come. I'd honed the stats and finally felt like the team was working like a well-oiled machine. We also had a better handle on the other teams in the league, which was good, because top of the American League was the Blue Jackets, the team that'd crashed us four games in a row.

Cash slipped a hand around my waist, smiling deeply as the guys took their shots. Cash wasn't drinking. I think the situation with his dad had thrown him off for a while. I knew he'd ended up paying off his father's house just like he'd said he wanted to do, but he hadn't heard from his dad since. My heart ached for him. I could see the pain haunting his eyes. He wanted a relationship with his dad, but right now they were on two different levels.

One night Cash had wondered out loud if his dad even watched his games. I'd told him I was sure he did, but in reality, I didn't know, because I couldn't fathom a parent so out of tune that they wouldn't even care to. Cash was a gift on the field, a star in the league. I know I couldn't keep my eyes off him when he played. My heart hurt for Cash, because his past was so similar to my own. I understood his pain probably better than any other. A father who wasn't a dad was the worst kind of abandonment. The love of a parent was supposed to be so absolute, that bond was the strongest to forge us and yet for us, it was incredibly broken.

"Can we get your autograph?!" A group of giggling college girls sped up to Cash in the hotel bar, thrusting out notepads and pens.

"Sure." Cash's lip twitched up in that flirty way as he looked at me and then pulled me to him, as if claiming me in public. I liked the feeling that he was telling all these women that I belonged to him and they didn't stand a chance. I swear I watched the girls almost melt in front of me. One even gave me a glare, but I beamed, happy and content to be wrapped in his strong arms. I untangled myself from him and backed away a few steps, letting them have their moment with Cash, before the last girl, with fire in her eyes, pulled down the neck of her shirt and pointed at her breast.

"Could you sign here?"

My mouth dropped open and my heart sank. These

ball players were hounded by beautiful women. How could anyone resist? They were younger, more beautiful, wilder than me, I'm sure.

My stomach twisted painfully as I watched Cash take the pen from her hands. My eyes shuttered closed as I imagined him signing her chest, her eyes doing that flirty thing, his hands on her skin, her legs around his waist. Suddenly reality crashed down all around me and the wreckage was unbearable. Cash Greenwood could have any woman on the planet. Why would he be satisfied with Delilah Grey?

I'd walk in on them fucking in the locker room and my heart would shatter into a thousand pieces at my feet.

What was I thinking?

He was a ball player.

I had to leave.

Without thinking, I sped away, punching at the elevator and willing the doors to open before Cash could pull himself from the group of girls. The elevator doors opened, and I turned just in time to watch them closing on Cash's confused eyes.

Pain twisted in my gut as the elevator whirred up seventeen floors until I was safe and alone and in my own room again.

I fell onto the bed, my heart thundering as tears swelled in my eyes. Just as I was about to unleash and sob uncontrollably, thinking I was repeating the very same mistakes my mother had, a pounding echoed through the room.

"Delilah!"

"Go away, Cash!"

"Open this door!"

"Cash!" I screamed back, tears in my eyes. I didn't

know who I was angrier with, him for not leaving me to lick my wounds, or myself for pushing him away.

"I'm not leaving until the door is open, and you know what happens if I don't make that flight home tonight. No play-offs tomorrow. We'll both be camped out here until I'm a starved and useless pile of nothing on the floor waiting for you, Delilah."

I slid the chain across the door, then cracked it an inch. "I just need some time."

"That's bullshit. We both know what you want, and I'm damn sure it isn't you up here crying in bed."

"I told you, I have a lot of triggers. This is wrong. We're wrong. I know we've been saying that all along, but tonight just reminded me—"

"Tonight? What the fuck happened tonight? Let me in and tell me what's going on in that head of yours."

I shook my head as more tears welled in my eyes.

"Delilah." His serious tone pulled me from my breakdown. I locked eyes with his, and the way they bled compassion nearly unchained my heart completely. I swallowed, taking a deep breath and thinking I was in uncharted waters here. I opened the door and allowed him in.

"Now what the fuck was that about?" He entered the space, seeming to fill it up with his intoxicating energy.

"I just…I have issues with…stuff."

"I gathered." He crossed his arms, tipping his head to the side as he waited.

"My dad played Major League." Cash's eyes widened with the revelation. "For nearly three decades… My dad was Will Branch. *The* Will Branch."

"Jesus, Delilah. I knew your dad played, but…" He trailed off. "Over 2000 RBIs Will Branch?"

I nodded sadly, always hating this part. The wide-eyed, in shock, baseball royalty part. My dad had the leading number of RBIs in the entire league, and had maintained that record up until recently. Someone I knew was inching closer to that mark.

"Well I'm glad you told me, but it still doesn't make a damn bit of sense why you ran out on me."

"My dad cheated, Cash. My mom stayed with him for years while he slept around on her. He even picked me up from school once with a groupie in the front seat. I was twelve." That memory still cut deep. "He drank too much, he did a lot of coke, and he liked women. I'm just too afraid to repeat that, Cash. That's why I can't be with you. That's why every nerve in my body may be screaming yes, but my brain is telling me to stay as far the hell away as possible."

"Christ, Delilah." Cash circled me in his arms, drawing me close and forcing me to melt into him. "I'm not him. You know me. Up until now I've never even looked twice at a woman. Baseball is the only thing I loved, not booze, or drugs, or groupies. You've been with me all season. You know me better than anyone. I didn't sign that girl's chest, I signed a napkin. I would never disrespect or risk losing you. Don't you know by now that you are everything to me? When I'm with you, Delilah, it's like I'm home. When I look at you, I feel privileged that someone so beautiful and so smart would want to be with me.

"Loving you is everything, Delilah. You once told me that I wanted you because you played hard to get. But you, baby, you don't play hard to get, you play hard to forget. I am yours. I was yours yesterday. I am yours today. And it won't matter if you want me or not, sweetheart, because I will be yours tomorrow and for every other day that I take a breath. You are it, the missing piece, my perfect half. Without you, I am nothing, I have nothing."

"I... Cash..."

"I know, baby." He gently stroked my hair with his strong hands. "But you've gotta try, for me, for us."

Stray tears dripped onto his shirt, soaking into the fibers and leaving me breathless with all the emotions swelling within me.

"I'm sorry I ran away. I never should have done that. I just saw those girls, and all I could think about was my dad..."

"I know, baby. But I don't like you running from me. I need you running to me, then we've got a shot. I want to see you, and I want you to see me. I see all your bad and good parts, and I want it all. I love it all. I am a greedy man, sweetheart, I want every single inch of your heart, mind, body and soul." He placed a kiss on my forehead.

"I hate when you're so wise," I sniffed, wiping at a tear.

"I know you do." He laughed. "We okay?"

I nodded, releasing him from my grasp and sitting on the bed. "We've got to be at the airport in an hour."

"So let's get you packed." He paused when I didn't respond. "Hey." He tipped my chin up and placed a kiss on my lips. "I know this is hard for you, but we'll take it one day at a time. I can give up anything you need to make you more comfortable. We'll ease into this, okay? Time is what builds trust, and I got it in spades. I'll be by your side, or under you, but better yet on top or behind you." Cash whistled as he checked out my ass.

"You're kind of incredible, Cash Greenwood."

"So I've been told." He winked.

"You really didn't sign her boob?"

Cash burst into a laugh. "Nah, never signed a boob, though I've been asked a few times. I wouldn't mind signing yours, though." He caught me in an embrace. "Maybe tattoo my name right here." He placed a kiss right above my boob.

"Not a chance, Greenwood."

"What? You don't want to wear my mark?" His finger trailed across my chest to tease at the nipple peeking through my shirt.

"Maybe somewhere…a little lower."

14

Cash

Monday morning before Delilah was even out of bed, my bed, I was pounding out miles on the treadmill downstairs. She'd stayed with me all weekend after we had gotten in from our long flight, and this week was the start of play-offs. We watched games together, dissected plays and players, fucked like we would lose our minds if we didn't—and I was pretty sure I would—and spent every waking moment together.

I had to be at the field by one today, but I couldn't miss a day on the treadmill, so I'd pecked Delilah on the cheek, left her a note on the coffee pot because I knew that would be her first stop in the morning, as was watching ESPN highlights while I worked out.

Jogging on the treadmill got adrenaline coursing through my veins as I worked over the game in my head. I liked to visualize victory, imagining the plays and all the different possibilities. Just as I bumped up the incline, my phone rang in my gym bag on the floor.

I narrowed my eyes, wondering who in the hell would call this early. It wasn't even seven a.m., but I stopped to pick it up, anyway. Maybe it was Delilah telling me to save my post-workout shower for her. I would be into that. I was into anything with Delilah.

I answered on the third ring, prepared to hear her voice, but a stranger spoke. "Cash Greenwood?"

"This is he."

"I'm a nurse at Jacksonville General. Is Leonard Greenwood your father?"

A pit of dread formed in my stomach. "Yes."

"There's been an incident. The doctor would like to speak with you. Do you mind if I put him on?"

By the time I'd hung up the call five minutes later, my chest ached, I felt out of breath, and I was booking the first flight I could find to Florida.

I rubbed at the ache emanating from my chest as I rode the elevator up to my apartment. I opened the door and went right for my room where Delilah still slept soundly. With a gentle kiss, I woke her up, dreading telling her I would have to leave her.

"Delilah, baby?" She roused, smiling when she spied me. "I've got to go to Jacksonville. It's my dad."

"What?" She shot up, instantly awake. "What's wrong?"

"Alcohol poisoning. Someone found him passed out in

the front yard of his house. I've got to go. I'm so sorry."

"No, don't be. I can come with you. Just give me five minutes to throw some stuff in a bag."

"No, Delilah, the team needs you. Play-offs start in a few days and I don't know if I'll be back."

"Cash, you have to be back." Her eyes rounded. I knew I did. I was under contract to play, unless I had an injury.

"I know. I'm going to do my best, but I've got to get down there and help him. And you've got a job to do here. Do your best for the team while I'm away. I need you here so I can take care of stuff there."

Delilah frowned, her eyes burning into me. She wrapped me in a hug and I held her like that for long minutes, not caring that the car was probably just pulling up outside to take me to the airport.

I fucking hated leaving her. Now of all times, just when we were good, just when play-offs were starting, just when life was seeming to finally work out for me.

"Call me every night, okay?"

"I won't be gone a minute longer than I have to," I reassured her, kissing her slowly, trying my best to leave my imprint on her lips.

"I love you, Cash."

My heart thundered at her words. "I love you so damn much, Delilah."

We rested our foreheads together, sharing the last few stolen moments before we'd have to be a country apart. "Watch out for Rod for me, 'kay? He acts tough, but he really isn't."

"We'll be fine here. Go help your dad."

I stood, wishing she was coming with me. "You've got the keys right? Stay here. I'll feel better knowing you're at my place."

"Sure thing, boss." She smiled, trying to lighten my mood. I grinned, pulling her in for one last long kiss. "See you soon?"

"It won't be too long, baby. I can't spend too many nights without you in my arms," I said, leaving her all alone in my bedroom, all alone in my apartment, all alone while I went to deal with old baggage. All I really wanted to do was stay there with her and create happy new memories to drown out all the darkness from our pasts.

The car service pulled up outside Jacksonville General later that day. I threw my bag over my shoulder, then walked in, anxious for details on my father's condition.

"Leonard Greenwood?" The woman behind the desk typed into her computer. "Looks like you missed him by a few hours. He checked himself out this morning."

"What? I was just on the phone with his doctor. I thought they were keeping him."

"Well, this doesn't give me details, but if that's the case, he may have left against doctor's wishes. It's not uncommon."

"Christ, that old bastard," I grit, spinning and heading back out where I'd come from, hailing the driver that was just about to pull away. "1525 Casnovia, please."

"Change of plans?" the driver inquired with a nod.

"Something like that," I murmured as the car took off again, headed for my childhood home. The one I hadn't stepped inside of in over a year.

So much for leaving the past in the past. I was about to confront it head-on, and I had no idea what I might find.

"You need me to hang around?" the driver asked a few minutes later as he pulled up to the curb of my father's house. I looked at the ill-maintained lawn, weeds growing everywhere, my father's old Ford parked in the driveway.

"Nah, thanks, though." I handed him an extra tip before getting out, my feet heavy with dread. This place felt oppressive. I'd felt it as a kid, and it still weighed on me now.

My father had pretty much locked himself up in that place after my mom passed, and if I had to guess, I'd bet he checked himself out of the hospital to go have a drink.

I knocked once on the front door, hoping for a quick resolution so I could get on the next plane back home. After all, I had a girl and play-offs to think about.

"What?" my father's haggard voice called as the door swung open. "You gotta be shittin' me."

"Hey, Dad."

"You can turn right around the way you came from. Go back to that fancy life you got and mind your own business. Thought I told the hospital not to call."

"You were unconscious, Dad. They had to call someone."

"I'm fine." He shifted his arm, and I noticed for the first time the small amber bottle. He'd stopped at the liquor store on the way home. Not even noon and he was already wasted.

"I'm just here to help. Anything you need, you know I'll do what I can."

"Don't want your help."

"Dad—"

"Listen, boy, I don't know what brought you all the way down here, but I sure as hell know it wasn't me, considering you ain't been down here in a year."

"You can't even be bothered to pick up the phone!" I cried, feeling like I was twelve and we were having a row again. This was exactly why I hadn't come back. "I knew it was gonna be like this."

"What? You expect me to be grateful you came to play the hero, sit by my bedside and feed me soup?" My father shook his head. "You know things ain't been normal between us since your momma died. I made peace with it a long time ago. Can't turn back time, son."

"I never asked you for anything, you know. Not a damn thing," I grit between my teeth.

"Like hell you didn't!"

"Like what?" I challenged him as his hazy eyes swam back at me.

"You asked for more than I could give." He shook his head.

"Love? A father? That's all I recall ever wanting from you."

My father shook his head, rubbing at his forehead wearily, then swiped the keys from the counter and pushed past me onto the porch.

"Where ya going? What do you need? I'll go to the store for you."

"Not going to the store. Get out of my way."

I thought fast and pulled the keys from his hands, sending him spinning before he righted himself on the porch and leveled me with his gaze. "Give me my keys back, boy."

"I can't. You've got no business driving. You almost killed yourself last night, and you may do it again if you get into that truck."

"Bullshit! What do you know? You're never here, bailed on me the first chance you got."

The old man swiped the keys from my hands, shoving me into a porch beam as he did. I shook my head, following him when he reached his truck. I caught the door just as he was about to slam it, wrenching it open and doing my best to wrangle the keys from him. The old man slammed the door on my hand instead.

"Fuck!" I swore, feeling the muscles in my hand swell instantly. My catching hand. Jesus Christ this was bad, and he was so wasted he didn't even register that he'd done it. "Don't fucking do it, old man." I pulled the door open just as the truck roared to life. My father's eyes held mine for a long moment before he stomped on the clutch and threw the shifter into gear, backing out and leveling me with the driver side door as he did.

My head slammed against the concrete, and then everything faded to black.

15

Delilah

The first night Cash didn't call, I knew something was wrong.

The next morning, I woke up terrified. I had a feeling down deep inside that things in Jacksonville had gone horribly wrong, and it drove me insane waiting to hear from him. I walked the hallways with him on my mind, flicked through old baseball replays to try to distract myself, even did my best to keep my head in the statistics and try to make some projections, but it felt odd having Cash gone.

It just wasn't like him not to call. I hadn't wanted to be

that girl that rings up her guy's phone in the middle of the night just to make sure the damn phone was working, but I really wanted to hear from him. I really wanted to hear the smooth buttery tone of his voice. I wanted to hear that deep chuckle that radiated straight between my legs.

I wanted him to tell me not to worry, because that was something else I wasn't good at—not worrying. That's why I had a head for numbers. They were solid, no variables, work hard, see immediate results. It was comforting, but having Cash gone threw me off my game.

It was also driving Coach insane that he was gone. The entire team relied on Cash to be their leader, like a team captain, he guided the team. Everyone, especially Rod, was lost without him.

By the time the sun set on the evening of his second night gone, and after a few unanswered phone calls, I was on my laptop booking a flight to Jacksonville. I'd managed to get my hands on the player records and had scrounged up an old address that may have been his father's, or so I hoped, before I boarded my flight.

Now, immediately upon arrival, I was taxiing down the runway thinking I had to do what I could to get Cash safe and home and ready for the play-offs. I called the number listed in his emergency file, hoping his father would pick up, or that someone would tell me what was going on, but after six rings I was convinced no one was home and I was just wasting my time even being down here.

As I was about to hang up, the phone picked up and I heard a grunt.

"Uh, hello? Len Greenwood?"

"Who is it?"

"My name is Delilah. I'm a friend of your son's. I've been trying to get a hold of him."

"He's in the hospital." The phone went dead.

Hospital.

The hospital?

I choked on my sob, my stomach rolling with cold fear.

"We have to go to the hospital." Tears rained down my cheeks as the taxi driver nodded, changing lanes and turning to go back the way we'd come.

"Everything all right, ma'am?"

"No, no, I was a fool to let him go alone. Maybe I could have helped, and now he's in the hospital and no one even knew!" I babbled on, my heart aching with every word.

By the time I looked up a minute later, we were pulling up to the hospital entrance, and I was tossing twenties at the driver as I ran into the hospital.

"Cash Greenwood. Please tell me Cash Greenwood is here."

"Oh, Cash?" The first floor receptionist's smile brightened. "He's on the third floor. Let me just get his room number…" Her voice faded behind me as I punched the button on the elevator, cursing it for taking so long.

I waited, twisting my hands together as the elevator rose, bursting through the doors once it finally come to a stop on the third floor. Without even thinking to stop and ask at the nurse's station, I sped down the hallway, looking in every room, glancing at the dry-erase boards with patients' names on them. A few giggles came from down the hallway as a nurse exited a room. That was probably Cash's room. Only he could send grown women into a tittering teen-girl mess.

"Cash?" I ducked in, sighing when my eyes landed on him. He was lying back in bed, his hand wrapped in white gauze, a boot on his ankle. "Oh my God, what happened?"

"Delilah?" Cash asked, eyes wide as if he didn't believe I was really there. "Jesus, the hospital has been trying to call you ever since I woke up, but there was no answer."

"I was on a plane. I saw the missed calls, but didn't recognize them. And woke up? What do you mean woke up? Are you okay?"

"I'm fine, just a sprained wrist, and a pretty bad bone bruise on my ankle. And I have a bump on my head."

"God, what did you do?" I went to the bed, wrapping him in my arms and sobbing.

"My dad…" Cash's voice was laced with pain. "My dad hit me with his truck. I was trying to stop him from leaving. He was drunk,"

"Oh God, Cash. I knew I should have come. How are you feeling? When can you leave? And what about play-offs?"

"I'm gonna miss a few games, but the doctor thinks I might be able to play in two weeks. I'm hoping, anyway."

"Two to four I said. Are you the lovely Delilah he's been going on about?"

I turned to find a doctor in the room. "Yes, that's me."

"Glad you're here. He has been out of his mind asking for you. We're releasing him soon, I know he wants to hop on a plane and get back, but he's going to need your help."

"Anything, just tell me what to do."

"I'll have the nurse go over his discharge papers with

you, but it was a near miss. He hit his head. We were worried about a concussion for a while there, but he's out of the danger zone."

I listened as the doctor began talking to Cash, warnings about resting a lot the next few weeks. I'd almost lost him before we'd even had a chance to start; we'd nearly lost it all.

"Mr. Greenwood?" A nurse popped her head in, interrupting my thoughts. "You've got a guest. Okay if I let him in?" I shrank from her arched eyebrow. "You're a popular man, Mr. Greenwood."

"Sure, thanks, Mrs. McCarty." Cash's eyes grew round.

"Thanks for seeing me, son." I turned to find the old man whose voice I recognized from the phone call.

"You landed me here, I've got nothing to say to you." Cash's gaze was hard, frightening.

"Well, I've got a few things to say to you. I resented you, Cash. When you left, lived all those big dreams you had, I didn't handle it well."

I shrank back against the wall, wishing I could disappear, wondering if I should interrupt them to excuse myself. This was a conversation that needed to happen, I just didn't want to witness it.

"I haven't been a father to you." Cash's dad advanced farther into the room, his body slow and hunched with age and drink. He reeked of alcohol—he really was a barely functioning alcoholic. "I'm real sorry I couldn't keep it together after your mom was gone. I think she was the glue our family needed, and without her...I just let you go, son." I heard the tears echo in the old man's throat when he finally reached the bed. "I'm real sorry, Cash. I thought by staying away I was keeping you safe. I can't hurt you if I'm not around you."

Cash's eyes roamed up and down the old man's face, pain slicing his features. His eyes looked like those of a little lost boy who'd been hurt one too many times.

"I'm gonna stop drinking, son. I'm done." Cash's father paused, then turned and caught my eye. "I see the love for you in this woman's face, you know I've lived my whole life never realizing just what it was that made life worth living." He nodded, then turned back to his son. "It's love, boy. Love for your family and the love of a good woman."

Cash's fingers were twitching against the white sheet as he lay battered in the hospital bed, hit by the very man who was supposed to spend his life protecting him. I didn't know if Cage would have the courage to forgive him and move on, and I wouldn't judge him if he didn't, but I knew his empathy was deep.

"I'm checking into the detox facility they have downstairs. Nurse McCarty here was telling me all about it." The old man nodded at the nurse who had reappeared at the door behind him.

"Told him we can get him in tonight," Mrs. McCarty confirmed.

"I'm not asking for miracles, son. But I know I've done wrong by you, and I want to start doing right."

My heart almost shattered when I saw Cash's face turn up in the smallest of smiles. "That's all I want, Dad. That's all I've ever wanted."

"I love you, boy." Cash's dad leaned down, wrapping Cash in a weak hug and patting his back. I watched as Cash's eyes swam with some sense of emotional healing. He'd been waiting his whole adult life for this moment, and he deserved it.

I backed away, preparing to give them some privacy, but Cash stopped me. "Dad, I'd like you to meet Delilah."

"Hi." I smiled, feeling the heat of being caught burn up my cheeks.

"Hope you're gonna put a ring on that, son."

My mouth dropped open, and Cash started chuckling. "Have plans to, sir."

"After baseball season?"

"Before."

"Wait a minute!" I shrieked. "You're gonna ask me to marry you before the end of this season?"

"Well, now you've ruined the surprise."

"Cash! That's a few weeks away!"

"I know, I was wondering how I was gonna wait that long, too."

I laughed, shaking my head as happy tears streamed down my cheeks.

Cash pulled me into his lap, one hand in my hair as his lips touched mine. "There's no crying in baseball, Ms. Grey."

We flew back home on a red-eye, Cash was anxious to get into rehab since he still hoped to finish out the season. Play-offs were just starting, and while he'd definitely be missing the next few weeks' worth of games, he was hoping to play at least the last few, as long as the team got that far.

Depending on how the series went, he only had a handful of weeks to get back into playing shape before the Timberwolves would get their chance to play against the other leading team in the World Series.

"This boot pisses me off. Shouldn't I be walking on it to speed recovery?"

"Um, no. Not according to the doctor, you shouldn't."

Cash sat on my couch, baseball game on TV while he munched on sunflower seeds.

"Maybe I should get a second opinion." He tossed a few more seeds into his mouth.

"The doctor said you'll be fine, but you have to rest it." I lifted his leg gently, propping it under a pillow to keep it elevated.

"I can't stay cooped up like this, Delilah. You know, he could have taken away my career. I try not to think about it, just stay focused on getting better and be thankful that it wasn't worse, but it's not easy."

"I know, baby." I frowned, thinking how hard this must be on him emotionally. His dad and him had had the healing conversation in the hospital, but Cash had years of built-up bitterness to shed. "Keep in mind that wasn't really him, though. That was the alcohol."

"But it was him," Cash insisted. "That's the only father I've known, someone drunk and angry and dangerous."

"I know it's hard, but just remember he's trying. That's the best you can hope for, and trying is more than a lot of people manage. It's been a week, he's been calling regularly. This might be the thing that turns him around, Cash. Truly."

"I keep thinking that. It feels too good to be true, though." He pushed a hand through his hair. "I've been waiting my whole life for him to change. What's different now?"

"He almost lost his son," I reminded him. Cash's eyes peered up at me, swirling with emotion. Sitting on this couch had gotten him thinking a lot, and I wasn't sure that was the best thing. Cash was a guy who liked action, he liked to be doing something. Just sitting all day wasn't enough for him.

"Take me with you." Cash's tugged me down against his body. I wished I could keep him with me at all times. Him flying off to Florida by himself had caused this all in the first place. I knew it was silly to think that I could have changed the outcome in any way, but the fear that had clutched at my heart when I'd learned he was in the hospital had been like another side of hell. I never wanted to live through that again.

I wrapped my legs around his on instinct. "I'm pretty sure this doesn't fall under doctor's orders."

"I'm not good at following orders." Cash's lips brushed against my neck. I smoothed my hands through his hair as he captured my lips in a soft kiss. "Take me to the ball field with you today."

"Cash!" I huffed, pulling away from his deceptive kiss. "Stop trying to blackmail me into giving in. You've got a checkup next week. Don't rush it, or you might regret it."

"I'm going crazy sitting on this couch all day!" Cash locked my fingers in his and pulled me back against his lips. "The only bright spot is the fuck-hot nurse I lucked out with."

I grinned against his lips, succumbing to his touch when his hands raked down my waist and fisted at the cheeks of my ass. "You're not being a very good patient."

"Give me a chance to try better. I may have a bum leg, but I'm pretty talented with my fingers." Cash slipped a palm down the waistband of my pants and under my underwear. My heart hummed with love for him, his touch, everything about him.

"I've got to get to work, Cash Greenwood. Coach doesn't like when I'm late."

"Well, I don't like when you leave." Cash gripped my ass cheeks harder, dragging his teeth across my bottom lip and convincing me that being late didn't sound so bad right now.

"The field is weird without you there," I pouted, my heart falling when I thought of how much I'd grown used to him around every day. Sure, he was staying at my place while he rehabilitated, but I was at the stadium five or six hours every day without him. The job felt a little hollower without him around goading me. "I think Rod said he'd stopped by and hang out with you today."

"He's not as pretty as you are," Cash teased sliding a finger under the elastic of my panties. "Plus, all he talks about is Gina now. I'm glad he's found someone, but I think he handed over his balls to her."

"Cash!" I swatted at his arm, erupting into giggles.

"Call in and stay with me today." He wrapped a palm around my neck and pulled me in for another, deeper kiss. Our tongues swirled together, his fingers dancing across my skin, and the only thing in my head was that I wanted to pull off my pants and slide down onto him right there, window and work be damned.

"Rod will be here any minute, he doesn't have to be in to practice until later." I pulled away slowly, rubbing my body along every hard, solid inch of him.

A low groan escaped from Cash's lips as he watched me, his beautiful eyes dark with sexual tension. I turned, breaking eye contact and sliding my laptop bag over my shoulder.

"At least a goodbye kiss?"

I paused, pursing my lips at him. "If I come back over

there, I won't leave."

"That's what I'm planning on." His eyes did that sparkling thing I loved. He tossed one arm over his head as he stared up at me, the taut muscle pulling at his T-shirt. Stubble covered his jawline, and I almost found myself locking the door, crawling back to him, and ignoring Rod when he showed up in favor of lying naked on this couch all day with my strong, handsome ball player.

"See you later, playboy." I blew him a kiss, scurrying out the door before he could use his devilish hands and convincing words on me again.

16

Delilah

"Think we've got time for a quickie?" Cash's arms snaked down my waist, hands crawling up my thighs and pushing up the hem of my dress. His cold fingers dusted under the elastic of my panties, sending a flurry of excitement skidding through my veins.

"We definitely don't have time," I murmured, eyes glancing down the long, dark hallway we'd ducked into. "The guys are already warming up."

"They can wait while I make you cum." His fingertips glanced across the hot seam of my pussy.

"Cash..." I mumbled before his lips crashed against mine, our tongues burrowing together. "You should go."

He pulled away, his intense eyes burning with desire.

"You should cum."

I tucked my bottom lip between my teeth as his fingers swirled over my clit, one long finger sinking deep inside me. The cold wall at my back sent lightning bolts of frenzied lust through my nerves, my thighs shaking when Cash sucked the flesh of my neck between his lips. Razors sliced through my muscles with every overwhelming pulse of my release. Fingernails clutching into the stark white baseball jersey that hung at his shoulders, I shuddered. "Oh my God, *Cashhhh.*"

His fingertips slowed, and he removed his hand from beneath my dress and licked off each of his fingers. "Getting you off in public just became my new favorite hobby."

"I don't know if I should be worried or thankful."

"Mm, very thankful." His thumb dragged down my lips, the taste of me on his skin spurring new shockwaves of arousal through me. "Let's say we skip the game…"

"The World Series?" I giggled, curling a hand around his neck and pulling him in for a kiss. "Not on my watch. Go get 'em, Greenwood."

Cash gave me a cocky half-grin and stole one more kiss. Then, our hands locked, pulled us down the hallway and out into the vibrant stadium lights. The rumble of the crowd, like a living breathing thing, pulsed in the rows of seats above us. As we reached the edge of the field, Cash pulled me out into the dirt with him, giving a big wave to the crowd.

My heart pounded wildly as the crowd cheered, the opening lines of *Greenlight* pouring out of the speakers for their favorite golden boy.

Cash had come a long way to get to here. From getting wheeled out of the hospital a month ago, through hours of rehab and days of intense practices, he was sprinting and pitching better than he ever had, and I didn't even think that was possible. Cash was ready for this. He was born for this moment.

He turned to me, eyes sparkling with amusement as he brought my hand to his lips and placed a kiss across my knuckles. I beamed back, happiness pouring through my veins with every look he gave me.

"I love you, Delilah Grey," Cash murmured against my neck then dropped to one knee in the dirt. My mouth dropped open as my hands trembled.

"I can't believe you," I breathed, shock settling in when he reached into the pocket of his pants and revealed a dainty leather box. "Cash…"

"I know something good when it smacks me in the face, and nothing has affected me quite like you have, Delilah. I want to be the man who puts a smile on your face every day." He pulled the sparkling canary diamond from its pillow and slid it onto my finger. "Will you be my wife?"

I swallowed the lump in my throat, the crowd screaming and clapping around us, the smell of the dirt and the turf curling my insides, and him, Cash Greenwood asking me to marry him at the final game of the World Series.

It all felt so fast, and it all felt so perfect.

"Yes."

Tears streamed down my cheeks when he shot from his knee and wrapped me in his arms, lifting me in his embrace and swinging me in a slow circle. "You're my entire world."

Cash pulled away, placing another sweet kiss across my knuckles, the stadium lights refracting the large cushion diamond that occupied my ring finger. "Now everyone knows you're mine."

I grinned, wrapping my arms around his neck and whispering, "You're infuriating, Cash Greenwood. But it just so happens I like being yours."

With our hands locked, Cash escorted me to my seat behind the dugout, the people around my seat beaming with love-drunk eyes at Cash's little display. He was their golden boy, and now they loved him even more, I'm sure.

Cash had a way with people, the charm oozing out of him and drawing everyone into his energy.

I settled into my seat, pushing up my laptop as the game unfolded. Cash went up to bat in the third inning, and the stadium played *Crazy in Love* by Beyoncé for his walk-up song. I laughed out loud, watching Cash grin and send me a wave, then crouch down into his batting position. The first pitch landed outside the box, but the second Cash swung, following through with more power than I'd ever seen him use, and launching the ball to far right field, the ball clearing the fence and disappearing into the crowd.

Cash ran the bases, sending two more of his teammates to home plate in the process. The crowd jumped to their feet in a standing ovation. Two-five, Timberwolves were ahead.

I waited on the edge of my seat as the next few innings passed. Cash hadn't pitched yet, I knew Coach was saving his arm for the last few innings, if needed. At the bottom of the seventh, Rodriguez went out to bat, smashing another home run into the stands and running the bases with a cocky grin on his face.

I'd gotten to know Rod a lot over the past few weeks. He'd made a point of stopping over at Cash's almost every day, bringing dinner, talking baseball, spotting him while he lifted weights. When I'd first met Rod, he was all arrogant machismo, but getting to know him better had shown me a more tender side. And I was shocked to learn that he was still seeing Gina fairly often. It made me think he had a soft spot for her, despite the fact that he still talked about other women like a cut of meat. But something told me Gina was different for him, and that only made me even more curious to finally meet her.

In the eighth inning, the other team had closed the gap. With a score of 6-7, we were too close for comfort to losing the game, so just as expected, Coach sent Cash onto the field. *Greenlight* pumped through the speakers as Cash jogged to the pitcher's mound, his arms swinging when he got there. I watched silently, and as if the entire stadium had frozen, Cash threw his first pitch. A curveball that went wide before sliding back in, and it did its job. The batter swung and missed. Cash threw two more, and the batter swung and missed every time. I cheered and jumped on my feet when Cash struck out every batter they threw at him, until it was time for the Timberwolves to bat again.

I watched as Cage sat on the bench, the live feed on the jumbotron zeroing in on his angular face, hat pulled low over his eyes as he watched the field intensely. I wished his dad could be here to see him, but I had no doubt he was watching it on TV from his place in the inpatient facility. Cash and his father were working at mending their relationship, and even when Cash was busy in rehab getting his body where it needed to be, his dad called most days of the week just to chat.

I knew Cash was the happiest he'd ever been, his life finally feeling more balanced. The situation with his dad was something that had weighed on him even when he'd insisted it hadn't. The love was on his face, and right now he was intensely focused on the game because he loved it. He loved everything about it. He lived and breathed this sport, and when he wasn't playing it, he lived and breathed me.

I glanced down at the sparkling diamond, thinking how nice it would be to run down to the beach and have a small wedding once his dad was finished with his first ninety days. He was already like night and day from the first time I'd met him. I'd even talked to Cash's dad on the phone a few times, and I knew he'd really turned a corner, and hurting Cash, threatening the very thing Cash loved the most, had shaken him from the drunken stupor he'd been living in.

He was confident he'd stay clean this time, and just the way he said it, just the way he was so open and repentant, made me believe it was true. Cash and his dad taught me that miracles can happen, people do change, and love is all that matters at the end of the day—love for family, love for one another, love for the game.

Cheers from the crowd interrupted my thoughts as Rodriguez trotted to home plate. His walk-up song, *Black Betty*, made me roll my eyes, but I was cheering wildly a moment later when he drove a ball to center, sending a teammate to home plate and landing on first himself. Cash followed him up to bat, and as the crowd went wild, the pitcher threw him a slider that any player could have missed, but Cash connected with. Sending a long ball into the outfield, Rod scored and Cash landed on third.

I twisted my hands together, realizing this was the last chance we had to pull ahead. With zero outs, another teammate went to bat and sent a drive to left field, whirring past Cash's head before dropping to the ground. Cash ran for home, sliding in just a moment before the catcher landed the ball in his glove. The ump called safe and the crowd cheered.

Just as the catcher threw the ball back to the pitcher, Rod stole third, causing the crowd to roar. With one more inning to pitch, I started packing up the stuff in my bag and preparing to run down to the dugout and launch myself into Cash's arms as soon as he was done.

He jogged out into the field, a smile bright on his face before he seemed to land on something unexpectedly, his ankle twisting and a grimace of pain lacing his face. He recovered swiftly, and thankfully most of the crowd hadn't noticed, but I had. Something had happened. And I knew him. He wouldn't say anything and get through these last few pitches. He wanted to give the crowd what they wanted, and what they wanted was their star pitcher throwing the last inning.

I chewed on my bottom lip, frozen as Cash reached the pitcher's mound, his feet shifting back and forth as he was trying to work out the pain that seemed to be there. The catcher shot symbols between his legs and Cash made a few movements with his hat to indicate what kind of ball he was throwing. Cash was going with a breaking ball, something that would drop as it grew closer to the batter, causing them to swing lower than necessary and miss.

The catcher shot a few more symbols to Cash, telling him to go with a floater, but Cash and I had studied this batter, knew what he swung at, knew what faked him out. The breaking ball was the way to go. Launch it fast and watch it drop as it reached home plate.

I shifted in my seat, waiting impatiently as Cash finally looked away, his arm swinging back, the deft twitch of his wrist told me exactly what he was going to do.

The batter watched the fastball coming at him, seemingly aimed for his head, before he stepped back and dropped to the ground, thinking he was narrowly avoiding a ball meant for his head, when at the last minute it dropped and slid through the safety zone.

First ball.

I cheered, thinking Cash knew exactly what he was doing and what we'd spent the time studying. Cash knew his analytics about as well as I did at this point. All those late nights spent watching ESPN and talking about the players were paying off right now.

I grinned when Cash threw another ball, this time curving it far left. Then he threw the third ball, and the batter connected with it, sending it bouncing out to shortstop where it was caught and thrown to first to give them their first out.

Cash threw to four more players, only one of them scoring, when another batter trotted to home plate. Cash walked a circle around the pitching mound, loosening his shoulders, favoring his left ankle a little more every step.

Shit, he was hurt. Maybe I should tell Coach to pull him, but if I knew Cash, he wouldn't do it. He'd been prepping all season for this game and there was no way he would let a bruised ankle stop him from pitching.

I swallowed the lump in my throat when Cash threw another fastball, his gaze intense and his jaw clenched tight. He was in pain, I could see it on his face. He was pitching the best game of his life and he was suffering through it. Another curveball, and with only one more strike out, the crowd held their breath as Cash wound up for what we were all hoping was the final throw of the game. He twisted back, launching the ball as his leg twisted, the grimace on his face upon release all I needed to see. Without watching what came next, I launched out of my seat and made my way down the bleachers to run into the dugout.

The crowd was cheering, but I only had eyes for Cash.

He'd struck the batter out. The Timberwolves had won the World Series.

Players swarmed the field and were celebrating, Cash was enveloped in the fold of white-uniformed bodies as confetti and balloons released into the air. Camera crews flooded the field, microphones thrust in players' faces. I still couldn't see him through the swarm of people.

I had to see him.

Weaving through the sea of players and reporters, I came to the pitching mound, finally catching sight of his tall form in the sea of white.

"Cash!" I called, sprinting the distance between us, until his arm snaked around me and pulling me into a hug.

"We did it."

"You did good, baby." I kissed him on the lips. "How's your ankle?"

Cash's gaze darkened, though the smile was still imprinted on his face. "Little tender." He shook his head. "But we won the fucking World Series!"

He laughed, pulling the ball cap from his head and throwing it up into the air. I'd never seen Cash Greenwood more alive. I don't know what I'd been thinking avoiding him just because he was a ball player, because we lived for this game. I lived and breathed the ball field, knew my way around the sport as well as any of these guys, and it made me feel alive, too. I was wrong to deny it, wrong to judge the sport based on the bad experiences I'd had with my father.

Instead of denying my love for this sport, and one very special ball player in it, I should have embraced it.

Now I was.

I'd found myself again when I'd found Cash.

First Epilogue

Cash

"I can't wait to peel this off you later." I hooked a finger in the very low neckline of Delilah's dress and pulled the fabric down to give me more of a view of her beautiful tits.

"Hands off, handsome." Delilah swatted my hand away, and my dick throbbed anxiously.

"Listen, wife..." I pulled her against my body, grinding my cock against all that pretty lace and sucking her bottom lip between my teeth. "You made me wait a year to marry you, I want to enjoy the spoils."

"You're an arrogant bastard, Cash Greenwood," she purred, her teeth latching onto my ear and tugging. I dipped my hands below the soft curve of her ass, fisting at her pretty cheeks and anxious as hell to finally be alone with her.

"I'm *your* arrogant bastard."

"I wouldn't have it any other way," Delilah ran a hand down the front of my pants, making contact with my dick.

"Naughty Mrs. Greenwood." I dragged a thumb across the hard outline of her nipple through the pure white wedding dress she wore.

"Mm, I really like the sound of that."

"Which part? The naughty or taking my last name?" I growled. I liked her having my last name a hell of a lot.

"Both." I gripped her hips, prepared to lift up that dress and show her just how naughty we could be, when I heard a soft shuffle from behind me.

"Congratulations, son." My dad held out a hand.

I detached myself from Delilah, circling her with one arm as I replied, "Thanks, Dad."

"I know you've got big plans, I just wanted to say thank you for letting me be here. I can't tell you how much it means to me." Dad looked from me to Delilah. "I know you'll take care of my boy." His eyes looked watery when he turned back to me. "And you damn sure better take care of her, or you'll have to answer to me."

"Got it." I nodded, recognizing that he was using humor to divert from the emotion threading his voice. Delilah and I had both had a tough time with our fathers, and sadly hers had passed away before she had a chance to heal, but for that reason she'd pushed me to mend fences, and in all honesty, it hadn't been hard since he'd stopped drinking. He'd been sober for more than year now, and we were both so much better because of it.

"I know we've been through a lot, son. I'll spend all the rest of my days with regrets. I'm not sure if I ever told you this, but I'm proud of you, Cash." He smacked me on the shoulder.

He'd never told me that before. And in some small way I figured it was for the best. He'd withheld his approval and lit a fire under my ass to gain it. "I wouldn't be the man I am today without you, Dad."

He pulled me in for a hug, and as Delilah swept away tears as she looked on, my heart felt fuller than I'd ever known possible. She'd saved me from myself, her support and love the two priceless gifts I'd been waiting a lifetime for. I was sure life couldn't get any better.

Second Epilogue

Delilah

I clutched at his palm, my feet giving way to sand as Cash pulled me through the dark. "How much farther?"

"Shh, good things come to those who wait."

Wasn't that the truth?

We hit the flat ground, my feet shuffling through the blond crystals with less difficulty when Cash spun me, covering my eyes with his palm. "Ready for your surprise?"

"Born ready, Cash Greenwood."

"Happy anniversary, Delilah." Cash removed his hand, pulling me around the corner of an embankment of rocks jutting out onto the beach. A billowing white tent sat perched high on the shoreline, rolling dunes and sea grass surrounding it, the interior lit with dozens of candles emitting a soft yellow glow.

"This is magical." I stepped forward in awe, my fingertips tracing the wisps of white dancing on the beach breeze. "I can't believe you did all of this."

"The guys told me the second anniversary is big." Cash pulled me inside the tent filled with mounds of pillows, a large bed piled high with fluffy white linens that looked softer than a cloud.

"You are incredible. I'm the luckiest woman on earth." I wrapped my arms around his neck and kissed along his steel-carved and stubbled jawline. "I love you so much."

"I love you a thousand times more, baby. Don't ever doubt that."

"Never, Cash Greenwood." I hummed when he lifted me in his arms, laying me across the bed and pushing his hands up my shirt.

"You taste better than anything I've ever put in my mouth. You're the air I breathe, Delilah." He worked his hands up my torso, lighting fire across my skin. His nose trailed across my collarbone, his hands reaching for my wrists and stretching my arms above my head. "Sooner I get inside you, the happier we'll both be."

His hands tracked up my skin, my thighs shifting as arousal pulsed through my veins. Every day of the last year had been like walking through a dream. If it was possible, Cash was even more thoughtful and attentive than I'd ever even realized.

"I'd spend every day on my knees in the sand with you, Mrs. Greenwood," he confided, trailing his lips across my abdomen until his hands were shoving up the hem of my skirt. His nose brushed over the seam of my pussy, and a fevered shiver coursed through me.

My fingers threaded in his hair as his teeth caught the elastic of my panties and he pulled them down my legs. "Even sweeter than sweet tea."

I moaned when his tongue trailed up my pussy, caressing the nerves and sending me shaking with mad, wild, desperate lust. I groaned when I heard the sound of his zipper lowering, his arms catching behind my knees as he sucked the bud of my clit and sent stars exploding into my vision. I pulsed and quaked, feeling like every heady current of pleasure running through my body would never end. Before I'd even come down from my first orgasm, Cash was pushing into me, his hard, heavy cock pushing past every ragged nerve I possessed, prolonging my climax.

"Oh my God, I love you," I groaned when he leaned down, sucking my nipple through the fabric of my bra, his teeth nipping and teasing at the heated flesh.

"You were made for me, Delilah. Every inch of this body was made to be pleased by me, that smart mouth of yours made to turn me on and drive me in*fuckings*ane. Everything about you makes me crazy and I can't get enough." He angled his hips and punctuated his words with the heavy thrusts. I clutched at his shoulders when he pushed me to the very edge, his thumb swirling between us, making me scream with raw pleasure.

"You're everything I never wanted, Cash Greenwood, and the best decision I ever made." I caught his lip between my teeth, tugging hard enough to cause a growl to escape from his full lips.

"Jesus, Delilah." His grip tightened at my hips as he shuddered, the muscles in his body tense as he came deep inside me. "I love when you're covered in sweat, sex and me." Cash pulled his cock from me, swiping at the fluid that leaked out between my thighs as he did. Swirling the glistening arousal over my stomach, he grinned, shoving one finger into my mouth and forcing me to suck.

"Everything about you surprises me." He lay next to me, hands covering my warm skin and making endorphins charge through my system at full speed.

"Didn't I mention I had a surprise, too?" My stomach flipped. I hadn't planned to tell him until tomorrow night over a candlelit dinner, but now seemed perfect.

"You surprise me every day." He trailed a fingertip around my navel. "You didn't need to get me anything."

"It's something for both of us." I bit down on my lip, glancing from his hand holding my stomach, then back to his eyes. His gaze flickered, landing on his hand as emotion flooded his irises and he looked back to me.

"You're not...? Are we having a baby?" Unable to form words, I nodded, choking on a lump of happy tears. "Oh my God, baby." He gathered me in his arms, raining kisses on my cheeks as he held me, rocking us both back and forth. Then I felt a few drops of moisture on my cheeks. Tears trickled down Cash's beautiful face. My strong, handsome, beautiful man was crying because he was so overjoyed to be a father. Cash was going to be a dad.

"I just found out this morning. I didn't know how I was going to keep it from you. We're pregnant, Cash."

"I didn't think my life could get any better, Delilah. Marrying you two years ago made me the happiest man alive, but you making me a daddy...." He shook his head, his grin brilliant. "Look, you've turned me into a sap."

"You always were a sap, Greenwood, but your secret is safe with me," I teased, running my fingers through his hair as he pushed me back down into the pillows and covered his lips with mine.

Cash had walked into my life and turned it completely upside down. He was exactly what I needed.

Third Epilogue

Cash

"Delilah!" I called at the top of my lungs.

"What?!" My beautiful wife came around the corner, our daughter bouncing joyously on her hip.

"Did you see that? Think you can do it again, Cade?" I cooed to my three-year-old son. His toothy smile undid my heart. "Here we go." I tossed the soft ball to my boy and watched as he caught it in both chubby hands.

Delilah whooped, and Daphne's pigtails glinted in the bright sunlight as she clapped.

"Good job, man!" I swung Cade into my arms and joined his mom and sister at the corner of the house. "Think we got a ball player, Mama."

"Well, he's got it in his genes." Delilah placed a kiss on his cheek.

"I think this little lady is gonna have a head for numbers. We could work on creating a whole team, whaddya say?" I grinned, stealing a kiss from Delilah.

"We've got a ways to go," she laughed.

"Three down." I winked, rubbing at the small bump already rounding her belly.

"Grandpa!" Cade squirmed out of my arms and dropped to his feet in the grass, barreling full-speed across the lawn to my father. He grinned, bending down and wrapping my son in a hug.

"Hey, Dad!"

"Hey, kids!" he called, waving at Delilah and reaching deep into his pocket and pulling out a silver dollar for Cade.

"Woah!" His eyes were wide as my father explained how precious the coin was. I think I heard something about pirates, which was just like my dad, spinning tall tales for amusement.

We'd moved to Florida a few years ago, after I'd been transferred to a new team. I'd pictured spending my entire career with the Timberwolves at one time, but being transferred to the Sea Rays felt like a blessing after Delilah and I had started giving my dad the grand babies he'd been wanting so badly.

He'd been clean and sober for a few years now, and while his health had taken a toll on him over the years, he was still a spry old guy who kept up with my little ones just fine.

I grinned at Delilah, pulling her into me as we watched our little boy playing, our sweet little girl crushed between us and the next one only months away.

Life was perfect. Life wouldn't get any better.

I'd once lived and breathed for the game, but as soon as Delilah Grey had walked into my life she'd shown me every important detail I'd been missing. Delilah gave me love, and with her love she breathed life into me.

Life was made up of a series of moments, and every one of them with her was more beautiful than the last.

Fourth Epilogue

Delilah

"That's him? Number eight, right?" I squealed, bopping up and down in my seat as I clutched at Cash's arm.

Cash chuckled next to me, his eyes darting from the field, then back to me. "That's number 18. He's warming up in the bullpen." Cash nodded, directing my attention across the field to my son, rookie pitcher in the Major League.

Just like his daddy.

I burrowed into Cash's arm, enjoying the warmth of his body curled around me, even after all these years. Our lives had changed a lot over the years, the salt and pepper in his stubble and at his temples proving that men did age very well. I got a little older, but Cash was still able to make me feel like a teenage girl with a crush on the most handsome boy in school. I never thought it was possible, but as time went by, I loved Cash even more. Every day I woke up happy that my life had turned out the way it had.

Cash had retired from the major league just in time to coach Cade's little league career. We'd soon realized that our son had a natural talent for the game, not that it was surprising. The kid was practically born with a mitt on his hand, and his swing was out of this world.

He'd already smashed the highest record at the farm club he'd played with, and it hadn't taken them long to call him up to play with the team.

"He's coming!" I clutched Cash's knee as our twenty-three year old son walked out into the field. Youngest rookie with the highest average to ever step foot in the MLB, the sports media was already buzzing, saying that he was bound to be a star.

"He looks good." Cash nodded, watching Cade as he walked to the pitcher's mound, loosening his arm with wide circles. "He's got this." Cash was so proud of Cade, not just because he played baseball but because Cash knew he raised a good, strong boy who knew that he had a father he could turn to and depend on. Cash had been a fantastic father. All the pain we had in our childhoods was nonexistent in our children's lives.

I smiled, love burning so deep as I watched the man I love cheer on the son he loved so dearly. This was a full circle moment, and one that was a thread through generations of our lives. Baseball had played a role in my grandfather's life, my father's, mine and Cash's, and now

Cade's.

"Delilah, he's pitching." Cash's voice was laced with so much pride.

I stopped instantly, eyes on my boy as he pulled his arm back and released a fastball the likes of which I hadn't seen in a long time.

Nearly eight years, to be exact.

"That had to be 101 at least, right?" Cash said next to me.

I laughed, shaking my head and thinking how in his element he was.

How perfect we were, still after all these years, right here with our asses parked in stadium seats.

This game had defined both of our lives and given us so much back.

Seeing Cash on the ballfield made my heart swell with an eternity of love.

This was where he was meant to be, and with him was where I was meant to be. Maybe it's true we don't know what we have until we lose it, but I hadn't known what I was missing until I'd found it. Cash had broken down my walls without me even knowing it and then built them back up with so much love that I felt invincible and finally strong. And twenty years later, with just one kiss, I still knew I was the ruler of his whole universe, because he ruled mine.

"It's a strike!" Cash shot up in the air, clapping like the proud ball dad he was.

I shook my head, grin turning up my cheeks as I stood next to my husband, clapping like a madwoman for my son, rookie MLB star and baseball royalty, Cade Greenwood.

Fifth Epilogue

Cash

I locked my fingers through Delilah's, pulling her a little closer.

I needed her now. I needed her every day, but for some reason today was especially hard. Today I was doing something no man ever liked to think about.

Today I was giving away my baby girl.

I knew that she'd found a good man who would love her the way I loved her mother, and if he didn't...well then her daddy would have to buy a shotgun.

"Cade just got here. He brought Lily again. I think she's the one." Delilah grinned as she approached me, waiting still as a statue at the back of the church. "He has to fly back out tonight. He's got a game tomorrow, but I'm so glad he could make it." Cade was killing it in the MLB. Five years in and he claimed the title of star pitcher for his team. He was now a free agent and demanded a high price tag for it. He'd broken salary records, too. The boy had a gift, much more than I ever did, though commentators liked to draw similarities.

I wrapped my arms around Delilah's waist, pulling her in closer for a moment. Our foreheads connecting, I closed my eyes and inhaled a breath of her comforting scent. Honey, lavender, pure sweetness, Delilah. "I can't believe this day is here."

"They grew up so fast." Delilah rested her hands on my cheeks, guiding my gaze to meet hers. "You look handsome today, father of the bride." She pressed up on her tiptoes, leaving a heartfelt kiss on my lips.

"I'm the luckiest man alive. Thank you my love. Thank you for spending your days with me, thank you for loving me. You know I have looked at you in a million different ways over the years and I have loved you with each and every look. You walk into a room and you still take my breath away. Thank you for making my life so full, and God bless you for doing the heavy lifting and giving me our beautiful children," I uttered, feeling like my heart was the fullest it'd ever been.

I knew if the new groom loved my darling little girl half as much as I loved her mother, she would be a happy woman forever.

"I love you, Cash. And if you ruin my makeup on my daughter's wedding day, I will murder you in your sleep."

"Is it too late for me to tell them I do not give this woman's hand?"

Delilah laughed. I was sure there wasn't a sound sweeter. That laugh had gotten me through a lot over a lifetime.

When I'd torn a rotator cuff and had to sit out a season, she'd been the only nurse I'd wanted.

When I'd watched her comfort our children late at night when they had a fever or growing pains, I'd known she was the right choice.

When my dad had passed at the age of ninety-two, she'd been there, holding me while tears burned behind my eyelids, knowing never again would I hear him call me *son*.

"We should have had more boys." I scrubbed at my face, willing the tears to stay put.

"You've only got to do this once." Delilah smiled softly, her fingertips straightening my bow tie.

"Once is all I'm gonna live through," I said, just as the doors to the small room opened and my daughter slipped out of the room, eyes meeting mine instantly.

"Daddy."

"Daphne." I held an arm out to tuck her into my body. "You look beautiful, sweetheart." I kissed the crown of head through the puffy white veil. A few tears finally slipped down my cheeks as I thought about walking her down the aisle in the next few moments.

Delilah caught my eye, swiping her thumb across my cheek and chasing away my salty tear tracks. "I love you," she mouthed softly.

My heart tore through my chest. Pulling them closer, I thanked the stars I'd been blessed with so much in my life.

"My beautiful family. You're my everything."

THE END.

Acknowledgments

First, I have to thank my ever so loving and patient husband. You truly are my HEA, babe. <3

Thank you to Aria's Assassins for keeping my fire burning. I am forever grateful for your love and cheerleading!

I can't thank the ArdentProse team enough. You ladies make my life so much easier and I love you for it!

To my ladies...the ladies that love to get lost in books about true and last lasting love... THANK YOU!!! Writing books you love is what keeps me going. You are my rock stars!

About the Author

Aria Cole is a thirty-something housewife who once felt bad for reading dirty books late at night, until she decided to write her own. Possessive alpha men and the sassy heroines who love them are common, along with a healthy dose of irresistible insta-love and happily ever afters so sweet your teeth may ache.

For a safe, off-the-charts HOT, and always HEA story that doesn't take a lifetime to read, get lost in an Aria Cole book!

Follow Aria on Amazon for new release updates, or stalk her on Facebook and Twitter to see which daring book boyfriend she's writing next!

⭐ Sign up to get a NEW RELEASE ALERT from

me!
→ http://eepurl.com/ccGnRX

More from Aria Cole:

☆ Sign up to get a NEW RELEASE
ALERT from me!
→ http://eepurl.com/ccGnRX

Made in the USA
Columbia, SC
03 February 2018